# Dan Turner

## Hollywood Detective

## No. 12

# DAN TURNER
## HOLLYWOOD DETECTIVE
## NO. 12

BY

### ROBERT LESLIE BELLEM

"Dead Man's Head", *Spicy Detective Stories*, August 1936;
"Silverscreen Spectre", *Spicy Detective Stories*, October 1936;
"Murder For Metrovox", *Spicy Detective Stories*, November
1936; "Death For A Name", *Spicy Detective Stories*, April 1937;
"Murder On The Sound Stage", *Private Detective Stories*, June
1937; "Death's Blue Discs", *Spicy Detective Stories*, September 1940;
"Crimson Comedy", *Spicy Detective Stories*, December 1941.

Published September 2025

isbn 978-1-64720-689-5 (trade paperback)

# TABLE OF CONTENTS

# DEAD MAN'S HEAD

Some one sends Dan Turner a gruesome package of murder, and his opening it plunges him into new depths of deadly Hollywood intrigue

I OPENED the package and a human head rolled out into my lap. A man's head—with a bullet-hole between the eyes.

It was late at night, in my apartment. I'd been to see Chaplin's latest picture at the Chinese, and when I got home I found a bundle wrapped in brown paper outside the door of my flat. I picked it up and carried it in.

There weren't any postage stamps on it; no express-tags, either. Evidently someone had delivered it personally. Printed across the front was: "For Dan Turner, private detective." That was all. No sender's name; no return address.

I cut the strings and unwrapped the bundle. And that's when the severed head rolled spang into my lap.

It startled hell out of me. I said: "What the hell!" and jumped to my feet. The head hit the floor with a gruesome bounce. It rolled half-way across my living-room rug. Then it came to rest, face upward. A damned nasty sight.

For a minute I was shaky as hell. I reached for a bottle of Vat 69 and tilted it down my throat. That made me feel a little better, but not much. I walked over and picked up the severed head.

There wasn't any blood around the bullet-wound in its forehead. None at the neck, either. That had all been washed away, nice and clean. I took one good gander at the white, cold features; and I recognized the face right away.

IT WAS the head of Skinny Arkle. Maybe you remember him. He was a big-shot screen comedian back in the silent days. Skinny Arkle had been even funnier than his name. He'd been tops in the old pie-throwing class, and the way he used to pop his false teeth out of his mouth and fold up his face kept the

*Sanston dropped the gun. "Good God! You don't think I . . . ?" he said.*

whole country in stitches. But at the height of his popularity, Skinny Arkle had got himself in a hell of a jam.

He'd gone on a binge down in San Diego with an obscure extra dame named Nancy Norward, He and the Norward girl had got plastered together—and the dame had kicked the bucket. They'd tried to pin her death on Skinny Arkle, but a jury finally decided she'd cashed in from acute alcoholism coupled with gizzard-trouble or something. Anyhow, they'd turned Skinny loose.

Just the same, the scandal had cooked Skinny

Arkle's goose in the movies. All the studios black-listed him; the stink had given Hollywood too much of a black eye, so Skinny had to take the rap—be the goat.

He'd faded out of pictures; hadn't appeared in a single film since the mess. For a while he went back to his native Jugo-Slavia; then he returned to Hollywood and married a cute kid named Kitty Calvert—a wren with red hair and a shape Iike seven million bucks. She was an Altamount semi-star, and she dragged down enough cookies in her weekly pay-envelope to keep herself and Skinny well fixed. For that matter, it was rumored that Skinny himself had salted away a nice stack of geetus from the days when he was in the big dough.

Well, that was Skinny Arkle's history as I remember it. And now, here was his decapitated head grinning at me from my living-room floor—with a bullet-hole in its brain.

I picked up the head and put it on my library table. Then I grabbed for my phone. I dialed the home number of my friend Dave Donaldson of the homicide squad. When he answered I said: "This is Dan Turner. Listen, Dave—something screwy has happened." I told him what.

Dave said: "For God's sake! Say—you're not drunk, are you? You haven't got pink elephants, have you?"

"Hell, no. This is on the level," I told him.

He said: "Cripes! Meet me down at headquarters in fifteen minutes. Bring that head with you!"

I said: "Okay," and hung up. Then all of a sudden I thought I heard a sound outside my door.

I was nervous anyhow. I had the jitters. I dragged out the .32 automatic I always carry in a shoulder-holster, and I dived for the door.

THERE was a tall, statuesque blonde bimbo standing there. I couldn't tell whether she'd just arrived or whether she'd been standing outside my door for some while. She looked scared as hell when I popped out at her. She said: "Oh-h-h—!" in a sort of muffled gasp.

I said: "Who the hell are you? What do you want?"

"I—I'm looking for Dan Turner," she answered me.

I looked her over. She seemed worried all right. But she was gorgeous, too—in a flashy sort of way. Her blonde head came above my shoulder, and I'm over six-feet-two. At a guess I'd say she was close to thirty—but she wore a damned good make-up that made her look younger. And her figure was something to remember.

She wasn't skinny, like a lot of tall dames. She wasn't too hefty, either. Just well-proportioned for her size. Sleek hips and slinky thighs. Breasts that would have been mammoth on a smaller cutie, but exactly right for this dame. Nice, firm mounds of breasts.

I said: "Well, kiddo, I'm sorry you're worried, but I haven't got time to talk to you now. See me at my office tomorrow."

She said: "No! You've got to listen to me right now, Mr. Turner! You must!"

I thought of my date with Donaldson at head-quarters in fifteen minutes. I said: "Sorry, sister. You'll have to excuse me."

"You—you mean you won't listen to me?"

"Sure I'll listen to you. Tomorrow."

Her eyes got sort of wild-looking. She said: "I'll *make* you listen!" And before I could stop her she rumpled her yellow hair and ripped at the front of her dress. She said: "I'll scream and tell people you attacked me!"

"Hell!" I said. "If it's that important, go ahead and spill your story. But cover yourself up or maybe I'll begin to get ideas—and then you'll have something to scream about." I reached over and pulled her frock together, covering her breasts. My fingers were tingling at the near contact.

The girl said: "I—I'm Constance Calvert. I'm Kitty Calvert's sister. Kitty Calvert, the Altamount star. She's Skinny Arkle's wife."

I stiffened. "Yeah?"

"Yes. And I'm worried for Kitty. Afraid for her. Skinny Arkle and she have had a terrible row. Skinny left after the fight. That was three days ago.

*I took one gander and recognized the face.*

He left, threatening to come back and m-murder

Kitty. We haven't seen him since, but I'm frightened. I want you to find him—"

I grabbed her by the arm and said: "Come on in my apartment. I want to show you something. You won't have to worry about Skinny Arkle any more."

I PULLED her into my living-room. She saw Skinny Arkle's severed head on my table. She went white. "Oh, my God!" she choked. And then damned if she didn't faint!

She fell sprawling on the floor, and the torn front of her dress gaped open. Her breasts bulged half out of the ripped frock.

I said: "What the hell—!" and leaned over her, lifted her up. I carried her into the next room, put her on the divan. She was dead to the world. I didn't know how long it would take me to bring her around—but I didn't have time, just then. I had to scram down to headquarters to keep my date with Donaldson.

On the other hand it struck me that this blonde baby, Constance Calvert, might be a key to the whole business. It was stretching the long leg of co-incidence to think she had just accidentally come to me the same night I'd received Arkle's decapitated noggin. She was mixed up in the deal some way. Maybe she was the one who'd brought that package and left it at my door!

Well, I couldn't take her down to headquarters

with me. Not when she was unconscious. But I didn't want her to get away. So I used a trick I'd pulled many a time before.

I stripped the dress off her limp form, and took her shoes and chiffon stockings off while I was at it. Fumbling around with her silk garters made my fingers itch. But I stuck to my job without any monkey-business, and pretty soon I had her down to her black lace panties, and brassiere.

She was a hell of a sweet number, there on my divan with practically nothing on. Her skin was as smooth and warm as new cream, and she had what it takes to drive a man utsnay. But I didn't have time to be driven utsnay, so I covered her with a blanket and left her.

I carried her duds out with me. I picked up Skinny's head, wrapped it in the brown paper, and went down to my jalopy. Then I drove to beat hell.

DAVE DONALDSON was waiting for me outside headquarters. We went into his office and I showed him the head. He said: "For Cripes' sake! It's Arkle, all right. Now, who in hell—?"

I said: "Wait a minute. Don't pop off with a lot of screwy questions. Don't ask me why this damned thing was delivered to my apartment That's one goofy thing I don't pretend to understand. But I've got a theory about Skinny Arkle's death."

Donaldson said: "A theory?"

"Yes. Now listen. Arkle was married to a girl named Kitty Calvert. Kitty has a sister, Constance Calvert. Well, just as I was starting downtown to meet you, Constance came to my door. She's a tall, blonde bimbo with plenty of sex-appeal."

"The hell with that," Donaldson grunted. "What did she want?"

"She claimed she was scared for her sister," I said. "She said Kitty and Skinny Arkle had a hell of a row three days ago. Skinny threatened Kitty's life. Then he took it on the lam and hasn't been seen since."

"So what?" Donaldson rasped.

"So this. Maybe Constance Calvert's story was a frame-up. Maybe her sister did have a fight with Skinny; and maybe Kitty shot the poor devil. Then maybe Kitty sent her sister to see me."

"What for?"

I said: "To cover the murder. To make it look as if they didn't know where Skinny had gone to."

Donaldson said: "Yeah. Sounds reasonable, maybe. Except I still don't see why they'd send Arkle's head to you."

I said: "I don't think Kitty or her sister knew the head was being sent to me. Maybe it was brought by somebody who knew of the murder and wanted to tip it off."

Donaldson said: "Where is Kitty Calvert's sister now?"

"In my apartment. She won't get away."

He said: "Wait till I turn this head over to the medical examiner. Then we'll go see Kitty."

He was gone about two minutes. Then we went out and piled into my jalopy. I drove—and I didn't spare the speedometer. Pretty soon we parked outside the Arkle home in Westwood.

I NOTICED another machine standing at the curb a couple of doors away. It was a big, shiny maroon Cad, and somehow I thought I recognized it. But I couldn't be sure, and there was no point in checking it up just then. Donaldson and I went up to the porch of the Arkle house and rang the bell.

A cute little Chink maid opened up. I said: "We want to see Mrs. Arkle, please."

The Chink maid spoke perfect English. American-born, probably. She said: "Miss Kitty Calvert has retired, sir. You'll have to come in the morning."

Dave Donaldson shoved me aside and flashed his badge. "We'll see her now!" he growled.

The maid widened her slanted eyes. "But—there's someone with—" she started to say. Then she stopped and blushed a little.

I said: "Somebody with her, eh? A man?"

"I—I don't know anything about it, sir," the Chink dame said. I could tell she was lying. Her left hand sort of fluttered toward her heart, covering the tiny mound of her breast through her uniform.

Donaldson didn't waste any more time. He

pushed the Oriental girl aside and said: "Come on, Turner." He ran up the stairs. I followed him. And then, just as we reached the second floor, I heard a shot.

I said: "What the hell—!" and made a dive for a closed door. The shot had sounded from within the room beyond that door. I jammed into it with my shoulder, burst it open. I had my .32 automatic in my fist. I leaped into the room, with Donaldson at my heels.

The room was all done in pink, with a pink-shaded lamp glowing in one corner. I sniffed the scent of expensive perfume. But I smelled something else, too. It was the acrid odor of powder-smoke.

IN one second I caught the whole scene. There on the bed lay a nude woman a girl. A girl with red hair and the prettiest breast I ever saw. The prettiest legs, too. An absolute knockout. It was Kitty Calvert— Skinny Arkle's wife.

She was as dead as a smoked fish,

There was a bullet-hole in her breast, right over the heart. She'd been shot plumb center. And where she was shot there was a round red hole, with blood seeping out of it.

Directly beyond the bed I saw a man standing. He had his coat and vest off, and he was in his stocking feet. He looked white as hell. And he had a roscoe in his mitt.

I recognized him. He was Billy Sanston—a big-shot director for Altamount Studios. In fact, he directed all Kitty Calvert's productions. And now I knew where I'd seen that maroon Cad before—the one that was parked downstairs. It was Sanston's own Cad. I'd seen him driving it many a time.

Donaldson said: "You murdering son of a—" and took aim at Sanston. "Drop that gun, you louse!"

*She went white and damned if she didn't faint.*

Sanston dropped the gun. It hit the floor. He said; "Good God—you don't think I—?"

Donaldson said: "I don't think anything. If you've got anything to say, save it for your lawyers. Stick out your fins for the nippers."

The movie director staggered a little. "But—but you can't arrest me for something I didn't do! My God, I'll be ruined! My wife will divorce me—I'll lose my job—"

"You should have thought of that before. You been playing around with Kitty Calvert, haven't you?"

Sanston flushed. "Y-yes. But—but I didn't kill her; I swear I didn't! I was here with her tonight. I admit that. I—I got up and went into the next room for a minute. Then I heard a shot. I ran in here and saw Kitty on the bed. She was dead; the gun was beside her. I—I picked it up, and then you men broke in. She—she must have shot herself—"

"Nuts!" Donaldson growled. "Come on—or shall I sock you on the dome with the soft end of my roscoe?"

Sanston swayed toward us, holding out his hands for the bracelets. Then he pulled an unexpected stunt. With his left he smashed Dave Donaldson's service .38 aside. Then he planted a haymaker on Donaldson's jaw. Dave went down.

I leaped at Sanston, but he got away from me. He scooped up the gat he had dropped. I drew a bead on him, pulled my trigger. But like a damn' fool I'd forgotten to unlatch the safety on my automatic. When I squeezed the trigger, nothing happened.

And by that time, Billy Sanston was out of the room and pelting hell-forleather down the stairs.

I HURLED myself after him. Behind me I heard Donaldson getting on his feet. Dave was cursing and staggering along in my trail. I hit the stairs, started down. But Sanston had a good start. Before I was half-way down I heard the front door slam shut. It slammed so hard that the glass shattered. I knew damned well that Sanston was out of the house.

I yelled: "You lousy rat.!" and took the last five steps in one flying jump. I jerked open the front door, raced outside. I saw Sanston in his maroon Cad at the wheel. Then two shots roared in the night.

I ducked, thinking Sanston was firing at me. But I didn't hear any slugs whistling past my ears. Then I noticed something queer. Sanston wasn't trying to step on his starter, get his car under way. He was sort of slumped over his wheel.

Dave Donaldson caught up with me. We both jumped for the maroon Cad, yanked its front door open. I said: "What the hell!"

Sanston was bleeding at the mouth—great, crimson gushes of blood spewing out of him. He coughed once. A nasty sound, the bloody cough of a dying man. Then he shuddered, stiffened and went limp.

Donaldson looked at the gun in Sanston's relaxed hand where it rested on the upholstered seat. The gun which Sanston had carried with him out of Kitty Calvert's boudoir. A trickle of smoke curled up from the gat's muzzle. Donaldson said: " Jeeze! He shot himself!"

I said: "Yeah. Maybe."

"What do you mean, maybe?"

I said: "Well, maybe he didn't commit suicide. Maybe he was murdered."

Donaldson looked at me. "Are you bughouse?"

"No. I don't think so. I'm just trying to figure a couple of things out. Listen—suppose Sanston told us the truth a minute ago. Suppose he was in Kitty's house, making whoopee. And suppose he left her for a minute to get a drink of water or see a dog about a man. And suppose while he was gone, Kitty was shot?"

"You mean maybe she really killed herself and he walked in and picked up the roscoe where she'd dropped it?"

I said: "Don't be dense, Dave. You didn't see any powder-burns on Kitty Calvert, did you?"

"No. Come to think of ít, I didn't."

"Well, then, she didn't shoot herself."

Donaldson said: "Well, hell! It was Sanston that killed her. Now he's bumped himself off because he realized he was out on a limb."

I said: "Not so fast. You heard Sanston say something about his wife? He didn't want to he arrested because his wife would divorce him and the scandal would make him lose his movie job?"

Dave narrowed his eyes. "By God! You think it was Sanston's wife—?"

I POINTED toward the side of Kitty Calvert's house. I said: "Take a look. There's a ladder up against the house. It's right up against Kitty's boudoir window."

Donaldson said: "I get it! Mrs. Sanston followed her hubby here, saw him making love to Kitty Calvert, and shot Kitty. But she didn't have a chance to shoot her husband too, because he was out of the room a minute, and when he came back we busted in. So she laid for him out here by his car. Huh?"

"At least that's a theory," I said. "It matches with the ladder against the window."

Dave said: "Then we've got to get Mrs. Sanston, by God! Maybe she's still around here somewhere. Come on—let's start searching!"

Even as he spoke, I heard the sound of a motor roaring from somewhere around the next corner. I said: "If it was Mrs. Sanston she's making her getaway right now. She'll probably go home to establish an alibi for herself."

"Alibi, hell!" Dave Donaldson roared. "Ill catch her! I'll put the collar on her and sweat the truth out of her!"

I said: "Go ahead. Use my jalopy. I'll go back in the house and phone headquarters to come and take the two corpses away."

So Dave got into my coupe and got going. I went back into the house. I picked up the phone, notified headquarters what had happened. When I hung up, 1 thought I heard somebody tiptoeing in the back of the place. Funny thing about people trying to sneak around without making any noise. You'll notice it quicker than you'll notice ordinary footsteps.

I made a flying dive for the dining-room where I'd heard the sound. Then I saw the Chink maid. She was trying to get out through a French window.

I jumped for her, grabbed her. She was trying to stuff something down the neck of her dress. I got my fingers into the vee of her uniform and yanked. The material tore. I ripped at the dress until something fluttered to the floor from between her tiny breasts. I grabbed it. It was an oblong of yellow paper.

The Chink girl tried to grab it from me. I slapped her across the face, pinioned her slim wrists with one hand. Then I looked at the slip of yellow paper. It was a check. It was made out to Miss Violet Chang, and it was signed: "Rodney Arkle." That had been Skinny Arkle's real name. The check was for five hundred smacks.

I said: "Where the hell did you get this?"

"Mr. Arkle g-gave it to me two or three d-days ago," she whimpered. She looked scared as hell.

I said: "What for?"

SHE closed up like a clam. Her red lips got tight. I knew I'd have to pull the cave-man stuff on her to find out anything. So I grabbed her shoulder' shook her until her teeth rattled and her tiny breasts jiggled around like cups of jello.

I said: "Now look, Miss Violet Chang. If you don't want to get mauled groggy, you'll talk. How would you like a good punch in the jaw?"

"No—no—! Don't hit me!"

"Okay, then. Answer me. Why were you trying to sneak out that window?"

She said: "Be-because I'm afraid! I don't want to get mixed up in this case!"

I ran my fingers over her shoulder, pretended I was about to pinch hell out of her. I'll admit I got something of a kick out of touching her. But I didn't let on. I said: "Why are you afraid to get mixed up in the case?"

All of a sudden the slant-eyed cutie pressed herself up against me, put her arms around my neck. She said: "Please, Mr. Detective—I'll do anything you ask if you'll keep me out of this! I—I have a brother who was smuggled into this country illegally. If I'm dragged into this shooting, the police will question me, look into my family. They might find out about my brother and deport him—"

She fitted against me like tissue paper. Her breasts against my chest, felt like little apples, and yet they were nice and pliant. She was offering me her lips.

Well, after all, I'm human. So I leaned down and kissed her ... felt her lips part against my mouth. My blood was racing, way out of control. I remembered seeing a divan in the front room, so I lifted the Chink cutie in my arms and carried her ...

IT was some time eater when I said: "Okay, baby. Now you know I'm your friend. Maybe you'll answer a couple of questions, huh?"

"Such as what?" she asked me.

I said: "Well, for one thing, how long had Billy Sanston been intimate with your mistress, Kitty Calvert? How long had he been coming to visit her?"

"A—a long time. Almost a year. N-now let me go, please—!"

"Not yet. Tell me something else. Did Kitty know Billy's wife?"

"Y-yes. Just slightly. They weren't good friends. Sometimes I got the impression that Mrs. Sanston suspected her husband of being in love with Miss Calvert. Of course I wasn't sure. Now please let me get away—before the police come!"

Outside, in the distance, I heard sirens moaning. I said: "Sure, kiddo. Put on a coat to cover yourself.

Then scram out the window."

She got a coat and I held it for her. I fumbled the job, killing time. Then finally I helped her out through the French window in the dining-room, just as the headquarters men rang the front door-hell.

I raced for the hall, yelled through the broken glass in the door. I said: "Quick—around the side! A Chink dame on the lam! Grab her!"

Those coppers moved fast. I heard them running around the side of the house. That was what I wanted.

For a minute I was alone. I set fire to a gasper and went upstairs. I didn't know what I was going to look for, but I figured maybe I might find something. I had three murders on my mind: Skinny Arkle's, his wife's and Billy Sanston's. I was convinced they were all murders; and I had a hunch they were linked to-gether some way or other.

FIRST I squinted around the boudoir where Kitty Calvert's corpse was. Then I walked into the next bedroom. It had been Skinny Arkle's room. I saw a desk-drawer open.

I saw an old book of faded press-clippings from the days when Skinny had been a big-shot come-dian. There were pictures of him in costume and in everyday dress. There was even a picture of Skinny as a kid with his family, back in Jugo-Slavia. It showed his mother, father, grandparents, a brother exactly the same age, two older sisters, and a couple of uncles and aunts. But I didn't take the scrap-book, It was too big, too bulky.

Then I found an empty book of check-stubs. I looked at the last three stubs. One showed that check for five yards drawn to the Chink maid, Violet Chang. The second said: "Pasadena Hospital, $250.00, in full." The third was to cash—for fifty grand!

Before I could look around any further, I heard a hell of a rumpus down below. The headquarters men had put the nab on the Chinese girl. I didn't want them to catch me going through Skinny Arkle's things, so I went downstairs on the run. I said: "You guys better take that girl to the jug. I think she knows something. And how about lending me a car for a while? Dave Donaldson took my hack."

One of the dicks said: "All right. Use the red roadster, Mr. Turner. Run it back to headquarters when you get through with it."

I went out, got into the red roadster. I drove back to my apartment. Just as I parked outside my budding, I saw somebody in the entrance. Somebody in a suit that looked familiar.

It was one of my own suits!

I said: "What the hell!" and jumped for the guy. I grabbed him. Only it wasn't a him; it was a her. It was the blonde bimbo, Constance Calvert.

She fought at me. She said: "Damn you! Let me

go!"

"Like hell!" I told her. "How long have you been out of my place?"

"I—I just got out. I found a suit of yours and put it on. Why did you take my clothes?"

BEFORE I could answer her, I heard brakes squeaking. I turned. There was Dave Donaldson driving up in my jalopy. He jumped out, saw me holding the blonde dame. He said: "What—?"

"Put the nippers on this girl, Dave," I told him. "She's hard to hold."

Dave slipped the cuffs on her. Then he said: "Turner, I've got news!"

I said; "What kind of news?"

"Well, in the first place," Donaldson growled disgustedly, "Mrs. Sanston had a perfect alibi. She's been playing bridge with friends all evening. Hasn't been outdoors. That eliminates her as a suspect. But down at headquarters I found out something damned interesting. Billy Sanston had been married before. His wife s name was Nancy Norward. Ever hear of her?"

I said: "Good God! Nancy Norward was the girt who died down in San Diego on a party with Skinny Arkle!"

Dave said: "Yeah. Now do you see the set-up? Sanston must have nursed a grudge against Arkle all these years. To get even he played around with Kitty

Calvert, Arkle's wife. Then, finally, he bumped Arkle off and decapitated the body. Maybe Kitty found out about it, so he had to kill her too. Then when we busted in on him in Kitty's boudoir he committed suicide. There was no other way out."

I said: "Dave, maybe you're right. It all checks up pretty well. Except one thing. Why was Arkle's severed head sent to me?"

"I don't know that," Donaldson grunted. "And there's one other goofy point, too. The medical examiner's report says that the bullet was fired into Arkle's noggin *after he was dead!* The condition of the tissues, or something. Look—here's the report."

He handed me a sheet of paper. I let him hang onto Constance while I took the paper to a streetlight. It was the usual formal report of the medical examiner—the description of the bullet-wound, condition of the flesh, color of the hair and eyes, so many fillings in the teeth, and the way the head had evidently been sliced from the body itself. I read it over once. And then, suddenly, had the answer.

I jumped back toward Donaldson. I said: "Quick! Get in my hack! We'll take this dame with us. And we've got to move fast!"

Dave said: "Where the hell are we headed?"

"Pasadena!" I told him. "The Pasadena Hospital!"

IT took us just thirty minutes to make the trip, and I thumbed my nose at a dozen stop-signs on the way.

I jerked all the tread off my tires skidding to a stop outside the Pasadena Hospital, and I grabbed Donaldson's arm. "Come on!" I yelled.

"What about this dame?" He pointed to Constance Calvert.

"Leave her here in my hack. She's handcuffed." I shoved Donaldson into the hospital and we went up to the desk.

There was an eldery woman on duty. I said: "I want to see a record of the deaths in this place during the past three days." Dave Donaldson flashed his badge for authority.

The woman dug into her records, handed me four or five cards. I found the one I wanted. it said: "Rodney Arkellmeister. Age 48. Male. White. Entered hospital in dying condition. Pneumonia. Unable to talk. Died two days later . . . " Then it gave the date of death and all that stuff.

I whirled on Donaldson. "Get it?" I said. "Rodney Arkellmeister! That was Skinny Arkle's real name before he came to America from Jugo-Slavia."

Dave said: "You mean Skinny died a natural death? Then who the hell cut off his head and put a bullet in it? Who sent the head to you?"

Before I could answer him, I heard a scream from outside. A woman's scream. I said: "What the hell—!" and jumped for the door, I saw a car parked behind my coupe. There was a guy leaning in my hack. He was choking Constance Calvert.

I said: "Damn! He must have been lurking around my apartment-house. He heard me saying we were coming here! He followed us!" And I hurled myself at the guy.

He heard me. He turned. I saw a roscoe in his fist. It vomited flame. A slug zinged past my skull. I whipped out my own automatic, thumbed the safety, squeezed the trigger. I sent three slugs into

*"How would you like a good punch in the jaw!"*

the guy's guts.

Even before he fell I yelled out to Donaldson, I said: "There's your killer. It's Skinny Arkle!"

Dave said: "You're crazy! How can a headless corpse get up and walk around—?"

By that time I was kneeling over the fallen man. I turned him over. It was Skinny Arkle, all right. I'd have known his face anywhere. Especially after seeing the decapitated head drop in my lap earlier that night, in my apartment.

Donaldson stared. He said: "Good God!"

I reached down, shoved my fingers in Skinny Arkle's mouth. I twisted—and pulled out his false teeth. I said: "Well, that proves it, Skinny."

Arkle glared up at me. His eyes were beginning to glaze. He said: "Damn you—!"

I said: "I see the whole thing now. You were the murderer, Arkle. You knew your wife, Kitty Calvert, was intimate with her director, Billy Sanston. You got proof of your suspicions from your wife's Chink maid, Violet Chang. You gave her your check for five hundred clams for telling you the lowdown."

Skinny Arkle gurgled in his throat and vomited a little blood.

I said: "By sheer luck, your brother had just come to visit you from Jugo-Slavia. *Your twin brother!* You and he were identical twins; looked exactly alike. I saw a picture of you two in your scrap-book a while ago. It showed you and your twin as kids back in the old country. You looked alike even in those days."

Dave Donaldson said: "I'll be damned!"

I WENT on talking to Skinny Arkle. "When your brother got to Hollywood, he was already stricken with pneumonia. You knew he was going to die. You saw a swell chance to murder your chiseling wife and her lover without being suspected of the crime. So you had your brother brought here to Pasadena—to a hospital. He died here. You arranged his burial somewhere—then you exhumed his corpse and cut its head off, put a bullet in it as a blind. That was the head you sent to me!"

Arkle said: "Ar-r-r-gh—!"

"You sent your twin brother's severed head to me, knowing I'd call the cops and notify them you'd been murdered. Then, tonight, you put a ladder outside your wife's boudoir and climbed up. You shot her and threw the gun on the bed alongside her, to make it look like suicide. Maybe you'd have shot Billy Sanstop at the same time, but he'd gone into the next room. Then when Donaldson and I broke in, you saw that Sanston would be accused of murdering Kitty Calvert—and probably convicted. So you sneaked down the ladder, satisfied. But a moment later, Billy Sanston escaped. So you shot him with a second gun you had on you. You shot him as he got into his Cad. That made it look as if Sanston, too, was a suicide."

Donaldson stared at me. "How the hell did you guess?"

I said: "I knew, the minute you showed me the medical examiner's report of that severed head. It mentioned several fillings in the teeth. And I knew that the real Skinny Arkle *had false teeth!* He used to take them out and fold up his face, in the movies! Then I remembered that check-stub I'd seen in Arkle's book—a check made out to the Pasadena Hospital. I realized the truth. Arkle had done the killings, and now he'd probably try to escape by going back to Jugo-Slavia on his dead brother's passport."

Dave Donaldson leaned over Skinny Arkle, felt in his pockets. He brought out a passport and a steamship ticket. That cinched the thing.

Skinny Arkle's eyes fluttered. He mumbled: "Well ... Turner ... they won't ... hang me ... you took ... care of that ... damn you ... " A spew of crimson gushed out of his kisser, and he folded up. And that was the end of Skinny Arkle.

THEN I remembered Constance Calvert. She was slumped over in my jalopy. Arkle must have followed us and maybe she'd spotted him. Anyhow he'd tried to murder her quietly, probably figured on bumping Donaldson and me, too, when we came out of the hospital. He must have known the jig was up. But I wasn't thinking about Skinny Arkle any more. I was thinking of the blonde Calvert wren.

She'd been choked unconscious; but she wasn't seriously hurt. I turned to Dave Donaldson. I said: "Dave, you stay here and notify the Pasadena police—have them take Skinny's carcass away."

Dave said: "Where are you going?"

I said: "Well, I took this girl's clothes off in my apartment earlier tonight. So now I'm going to take her back to her joint and put 'em back on her."

"Hell!" Donaldson growled. "I'll bet you won't hurry about it."

I said: "You flatter me, Dave." But it turned out that he was right, at that.

# SILVERSCREEN SPECTRE

It's impossible; but it's so! Dan Turner takes up the case of the haunted movie, in which an accidentally electrocuted wife comes back to plague her director-husband

SOMETHING went *"spang!"* against my coupe's bullet-proof windshield. A spider-web of cracks circled the shatterproof glass. It made a beautiful design, but I wasn't in the mood to appreciate it.

I said: "What the hell!" and jammed on my brakes. I slammed myself out of my jalopy and went leaping into the night to look for the bird who had fired that shot. But there was no trace of anyone on the sidewalks or the street. That section of Beverly Hills seemed as deserted as King Tut's tomb. The hour was close to eleven.

I saw that I had parked almost directly in front of Adolph Maenzer's home. Maenzer was a former big-shot director for Altamount Pictures who was somewhat down on his luck. Just thirty minutes before, he had phoned me at my apartment and begged me to come see him right away. His voice had sounded so pleading over the wire that I had agreed to call on him at once. And now, here I was in front of his Spanish stucco house—and some sharp tomato had pushed a lead slug against my jalopy's windshield.

From the direction the bullet had taken, I had a sneaking hunch it had been fired from somewhere close to Maenzer's joint. I walked up to his front door and rang the bell.

NOTHING happened for maybe three minutes. Then all of a sudden the door opened, and a little old lady peered out. She was short and dumpy, with a wrinkled face and a kindly, gentle expression. But right now I could see she had a grade-A case of the drizzling jitters. Her face was the color of watered milk, and she had a 1915 German-army Luger auto-

*I jumped; knocked the girl flat, as the gun in the window went, "Chow-Chow!"*

matic in her wavering fist. She was aiming the Luger at my belt-buckle as she opened the door.

I don't like people to point their hardware at me.

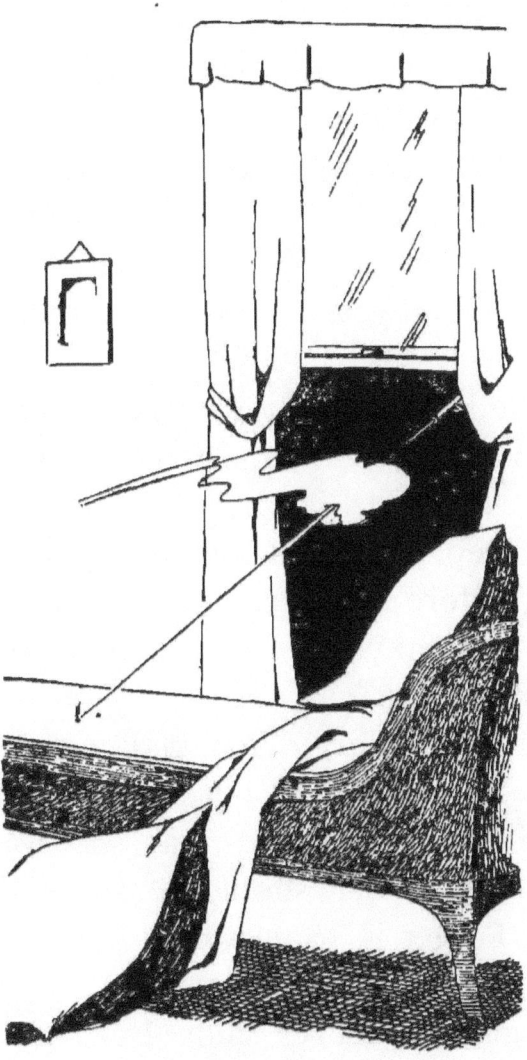

It makes me peevish. Besides, I'd been asked to come here. It got me sore to have a bullet thud into my windshield and then walk into the nasty end of a minia-ture cannon. That's no way to greet a man.

The little old lady glared at me and started jab-bering some-thing in German which I didn't understand. I saw her finger getting tight on the Lu-ger's trigger, and I knew I had to do something about it before she bored a tunnel in my belly. So I took a long chance and yelled: "Hey—look out! Behind you!" Then, when she started to turn around, I made a dive for her gun-wrist and twisted the big automatic out of her grasp.

She shrank away from me, whimpering. Just then I heard footfalls in the house behind her, and a man came racing to the front door from one of the rear rooms. It was Adolf Maenzer himself, and he was saying: "What's this? What's this?"

I said: "Take it easy, Mr. Maenzer. I'm Dan Turner. And I wish to God you'd tell me what this is all about."

Maenzer took the little old lady in his arms and spoke soothingly to her in German. Then he turned to me. "I am very sorry, Mr. Turner. This is Mrs. Hasdorf, my housekeeper. She has been in my family for years—long before I ever came from Berlin to Hollywood. She thought you were an enemy, and she was trying to protect me."

The wrinkled little Hasdorf dame grabbed my hand and clung to it. She sobbed out something I didn't understand; but I gathered that she was apologizing. So I patted her shoulder and said: "That's okay, lady. Forget it." She turned and tottered back into the rear part of the house.

When she had gone, Maenzer said: "I am glad you came so quickly, Mr. Turner. I have a very important investigation for you to make. I will pay you well—but I warn you, there may be danger."

I said: "Yeah. Somebody's already tried to put a

slug through me."

Maenzer's pan got sort of greenish. *"Gott!"* he whispered. His eyes started darting around in a furtive, hunted way. For some reason, he reminded me of a weasel—or a cornered rat.

Then he reached out and grabbed my arm. "Come upstairs, Mr. Turner. I will show you what has been troubling me."

AS I followed him to the second floor, my mind went over Maenzer's history—as much as I knew of it. He had been in Hollywood about eight years. In that time, he had become a top-flight director for Altamount. Then, about five or six months ago, tragedy and bad luck had commenced spotting him behind the eight-ball.

First his wife, a lovely blonde actress named Vesta Delorme, had died under shocking circumstances—and that's not intended as a pun. While taking a bath, an electric heater had accidentally fallen into her tub. There'd been a short circuit, and Vesta was electrocuted.

After that, Maenzer had gone all to hell. He'd started hitting the bottle, and it was rumored he also had tried a crack at the needle, too. In any case, he'd lost his berth with Altamount; hadn't worked for maybe four months—until just recently.

Within the past thirty days, a quickie outfit on Poverty Row had hired Maenzer to make one picture. He was supposed to be working on it now; and it might be the means of his getting a new toe-hold on success.

That was Maenzer's story as I remembered it. We reached the second floor, and he guided me into a leather-lined den. I noticed a small, silvered movie-screen set up at one end of the room; and opposite the screen I saw a projecting apparatus.

Maenzer said: "Mr. Turner, it is always my habit to view the 'rushes' of my pictures here in the privacy of my home. When a day's scenes have been shot, I have the negatives developed and prints made so that I may see the results by myself."

I nodded. "So what?"

His little rat-like eyes darted around the room. "Mr. Turner," he. whispered hoarsely, *"this latest picture of mine is haunted!"*

I said: "Haunted? What the devil are you getting at?"

"Wait. I will show you," he answered in his accented English. He switched off the room's lights and snapped a button on his projection machine. A square of brilliance danced on the silvered screen at the other end of the den. Then a movie scene splashed into view.

It was an em-cee-you—a medium close-up—of Carlotta Cordova, the Spanish star who was playing the lead in Maenzer's new picture. She was a lush brunette wren, with plenty on the ball in the way of tantalizing curves. She was going through her emotional paces in a solo scene as I watched the picture unwinding before me. And then, suddenly, I drew a sharp breath and said: "What the hell!"

*Somehow the hem of her dress had got caught in the rose vine, and she hung on the trellis, helpless.*

SOMETHING was happening to that picture on the screen before me. Carlotta Cordova was fading out, as if in a dissolve shot; then, replacing her, I saw the feature of someone else. Another girl. A blonde girl—

Vesta Delorme, Adolf Maenzer's wife who had been accidentally killed several months ago by electrocution in her tub!

Her image grew clearer, sharper, on the screen. She seemed to be looking straight out with accusing, haunting eyes. Then, as suddenly as she had appeared, she vanished; and Carlotta was back in the picture again.

Maenzer snapped off the projector, clicked on the room's lights. He was sweating, and his eyes were glassy. "Now you know what I mean when I say this picture is haunted!" he rasped. "Each night for a week, now, the same thing has happened! I bring the day's 'rushes' home to my private projector—and always my dead wife's face appears on the film! It is driving me mad, Turner! I'm going insane!"

"Wait a minute," I told him. "This looks like a gag to me. There are several ways it could happen. Your cameraman might be making a double exposure— filming someone who looks like your dead wife before photographing the scenes you direct. Or it might be somebody in the developing room who's superimposing an old shot of your wife on this new footage. It might even be a film editor or cutter."

"*Ja.* I have thought of all those things, Turner. And I have checked them. But the theory falls down. I have found out that nobody—"

That was as far as he got. From the door behind me, a shot cracked out. I felt a slug pluck at my sleeve and then plock into the wall beyond me, chewing out pieces of plaster. I whirled around. In my fist I still had the Luger automatic I'd taken away from Maenzer's housekeeper. I raised it and took a flying dive for the doorway.

The second-floor hallway was dark, but I thought I caught a flash of something white at the far end, in the shadows. I yelled: "Stand still or I'll let you have a load of lead!"

The blurred white shape kept on going; vanished through an open doorway at the end of the hall. I squeezed the Luger's trigger but nothing happened. The damned gun was empty. Even as I hurled myself forward, I sniffed its muzzle. There was no trace of burned smoke.

That told me one thing. It proved that Mrs. Hasdorf hadn't been the one who'd fired a shot at my coupe's windshield a while before. I dropped the Luger and dragged out my own .32 automatic from its shoulder-holster. I reached the doorway through which the blurred white shape had disappeared. I slammed myself into a bedroom.

There was an open casement window opposite me, and I heard a scratching, scrambling sound just outside. I also heard what seemed to be a muffled feminine moan of fright. I leaped to the window, peered outward and down.

The side of Maenzer's house supported a wooden lattice-work trellis covered with rambler rose-vines. There was a girl clinging to the trellis, just below my reach. She was dressed in white, and I knew she must be the blurred shape I'd been chasing.

BUT now she was in a hell of a mess. Somehow, the bottom of her dress had got tangled in the thorny rose-vines; and her whole frock was up over her head, trapping her. She couldn't wriggle her arms and shoulders free of the dress, and it was up over her face like a billowing tent, smothering her cries. From the shoulders south she was as naked as a picked goose except for skin-tight, glove-silk snuggies.

I couldn't see her face, of course, because it was covered by her updrawn frock. But I could see plenty of the rest of her. She wasn't hard on the eyes, either. Her squirming, kicking legs were plenty nifty; and the way her swelling hips filled out those snuggies made me feel years younger, made my mouth water. She was hanging by her hands; and her arms being over her head made her breasts pout out like taut marble cones. I noticed that she was losing her grip with her left hand; and when I looked closer, I saw why.

She had a gun in that left hand. A small, nickel-plated revolver! And there was a thin wisp of smoke still issuing from the muzzle!

I tried to grab her but she was too far below the windowsill for me to reach her. I said: "Baby, you're caught. And you'd better hang on where you are until I run downstairs and get under you to break your fall. Don't let go until I tell you, or you'll drop twenty feet and bust your pretty form."

She just moaned through the folds of her skirt.

I turned, left the window, raced out of the room and down the stairs. I barged out through the front door; but as I hit the porch I smashed into a lean, wolf-jawed guy who had evidently just come from the driveway alongside the house. We ploughed together like a couple of billiard-balls on a carom shot, and I went skittering sidewise. I recovered my balance, stared at the egg I'd bumped into. I recognized him. He was Barry Barkis, president of the outfit for which Maenzer was making a picture.

He knew me, too. He said: "Turner—what on earth—?"

I brushed past him. "No time to talk. See you later."

He grabbed my arm. "But listen—wait a minute—"

I shoved him away. I didn't like him anyhow. I dashed around to the side of the house and looked up toward the spot where I'd left the half-naked wren hanging on the trellis.

She was gone!

Her dress was still stuck to the thorns of the trellis; so I knew she must have managed to yank herself out of the frock and climb down to safety. Well, she couldn't get very far without her dress. I started looking around for her.

"A shot—fired from outside—for God's sake do something, Turner—!" Maenzer gibbered.

Before I could answer, I heard a motor being gunned to hell at the curb outside. I recognized the sound. It was my own jalopy! I said: "Damn it to hell!" and made a spurt across the front lawn, just as my coupe got under way. Then, all of a sudden I heard a sound that startled hell out of me.

It was a shot from inside the house.

I PIVOTED and sprinted for the front door. Just inside, I saw a sprawled form. It was Barkis, the quickie producer. He was flat on his face, and blood was seeping from a hole in the back of his noggin. His brains were splattered all over the place in a yellowish-red spew. Adolf Maenzer was standing over the corpse, looking sick.

"A shot—fired from outside—for God's sake do something, Turner—!" Maenzer gibbered.

Before I could answer, I heard a motor being gunned to hell at the curb outside. I recognized the sound. It was my own jalopy! I said: "Damn it to hell!" and made a spurt across the front lawn, just as my coupe got under way. I managed to catch my fingers in the luggage-rack behind the rumble-seat as my jalopy gathered speed; and I dragged myself up on the slippery, curved rear turtle-deck as the car went flying around the next intersection on two wheels and a prayer.

I peered in through the rear window; and I caught my breath. My jalopy was being driven by the dame who had clung to the trellis on the side of Maenzer's house. Now she was nude to the waist. I could see her gleaming shoulders, her coal-black hair. I caught a flash of her face in the rear-view mirror. I said: "For Cripes' sake! Carlotta Cordova!"

That's who it was, all right. The leading woman of Maenzer's latest picture!

I scrambled toward the left running-board as the Cordova cutie fed soup to the motor. She evidently didn't know I'd boarded the machine; because when I finally managed to reach the running-board along-side her, she turned and gave me one scared look. Then she said: "Oh, God!" and almost put us up on somebody's front porch.

I grabbed for the wheel, straightened it out. Then I jammed my automatic into Carlotta's neck and said: "Slow down and don't do anything rash, baby. Otherwise I'm likely to blow your head off."

She sobbed and cut down her speed to about twenty. "Wh-what are you g-going to d-do?" she whimpered.

I said: "I'm going to take you to my apartment and ask you some questions. And you'd better a damn' sight answer me straight, if you don't want to spend the rest of your life on the inside looking out!"

I KEPT her covered with my roscoe, forced her to drive to my apartment. When she parked in front of my joint, I reached inside the coupe and found her nickel-plated revolver. I shoved it in my pocket and said: "Come on, kiddo. Get out of there."

"I can't! I—I haven't any d-dress on!"

I slipped out of my coat, handed it to her. "Put that around you, though it seems a shame. Then we'll go up the back way so nobody'll notice your bare legs." My temperature went back to normal, with all that seductive loveliness covered.

I prodded her up to my flat, opened the door and made her go inside. Still keeping her covered, I managed to set fire to a gasper and pour a couple of slugs of Vat 69. I gave her one, drank the other myself. Then I hauled her down on my davenport forcibly and said: "Now, then, Carlotta. Just exactly what was your idea in trying to shoot a hole in my windshield when I first went to Maenzer's house? And later, why did you try to plug me when I was with him in his den?"

"I—I refuse to talk!" she flashed at me defiantly.

I reached an arm around her, yanked my coat

away from her shoulders. Then I looked her over. She was damned easy on the optics. Her bare legs were smoother than the soft pink silk of her panties, and her thighs were as white and creamy as a celibate's dream. Up above her slender waist, her lovely body swelled outward in two enticing little hillocks of flesh—and as an old connoisseur of feminine charms, I'd say that Carlotta Cordova was just about perfect.

She shrank away from me. "Don't touch me!"

I said: "The hell I won't touch you! I've got some questions I want answered, and unless you unbutton your tongue I'm going to work you over."

"I—I won't answer any questions!"

"Then I'll make you, by God!" I said, putting the accent on the *"make."* And hauled her against me, clamped my mouth over her lips, and started giving her the works.

She struggled and squirmed. "No—No—!"

I grinned into her flashing black eyes. I said: "Sister, I've got one certain way of making dames talk. It never misses. Now, either you spill the information I want or else...." There was no mistaking my meaning.

Very deliberately she laughed at me. "If that's your system, go ahead!" she taunted me. She drew up her arms over her head, so that I could see the smooth curves of her armpits and the contours of her breasts where they swelled outward.

I THOUGHT she was trying to run a bluff on me; and I don't fall for bluffs. So I kissed her again, hard. I was holding her by her bare shoulders, and my fingers strayed down her arms. She was beginning to pant a little.

I shoved her back among the cushions of the davenport and whispered: "Baby, either you're going to talk or you're going to be sorry...."

"You can't scare me. You wouldn't dare...."

"Wouldn't I?" I held her so tight that she couldn't get her breath. I could feel those firm little mounds burrowing into my chest as she squirmed in my arms. I couldn't tell whether she was wiggling to get away from me or trying to snuggle closer. By that time, I didn't give a damn.

I'll admit I'd started out just to scare some information out of her; but holding her so close and smelling the scent of her hair and feeling her warm flesh against me—well, after all, I'm human. I forgot my original purpose for a few minutes. What the hell?

THEN, when I thought she should have learned her lesson, I said: "Okay, babe. *Now* will you talk?"

She grinned at me. "No. I won't talk. And there's nothing else you can do to scare me, is there?"

"Yeah. I could beat hell out of you."

"You wouldn't do that."

"Maybe I wouldn't. But there's one thing I sure as

God *will* do. I'll turn you over to the cops for killing Barkis at Maenzer's house a little while ago!"

Her face got pale, and for a second I thought she was going to faint in my arms. "B-Barkis—killed?" she moaned.

I said: "Yeah. Killed. Bumped off. Rubbed out. And a half-minute after he was croaked, you tried to lam away in my jalopy. Now, how do you think you're going to explain all that?"

She grabbed me, held my arms. She was trembling so hard that I could see the quivering of her pert, perky little breasts—like bowls of moulded jelly. "L-listen, Mr. Turner!" she whispered. "I—I guess it's time for me to tell everything. I'll have to tell everything! And then you've got to help me send Adolf Maezner to the noose for murder. For *two* murders!!"

I said: "What the devil—?"

The words were gushing out of her now, like oil out of a million-barrel well. "This is what happened, Mr. Turner!" she panted. "A few months ago, Maenzer's wife, Vesta Delorme, d-died. Her death was accidental, everybody said. But I know better. Maenzer murdered her!"

"What?"

"Yes. I'm sure of it. In the first place, Vesta was my best friend. I 1-loved her as much as if she'd been my sister. And I happen to know that she had a deathly fear of electric heaters in her bathroom. She would never allow one near her when she was bathing. Yet she was killed by an electric heater falling into her tub. That doesn't make sense, Mr. Turner. You know it doesn't!"

I said: "Okay. For the sake of argument, it doesn't make sense. So what?"

"So this: It's my firm belief that Maenzer deliberately knocked that electric heater into Vesta's bath! He murdered her—just as he murdered Barry Barkis tonight and then tried to blame it on me!"

"Why should Maenzer murder Barkis? That doesn't add up right," I said. "Barkis was giving Maenzer a chance to come back. Maenzer wouldn't bump the guy who was helping him get back on his feet. That's screwy!"

"No, it isn't screwy. Not when you know all the details. You see—Barry and Vesta had been ... lovers...."

"You mean Barkis was playing around with Maenzer's wife before she was killed?"

"Yes."

"And you think Maenzer found it out, croaked her, and then waited for a chance to kill Barkis too?"

"Y-yes. That's what I think."

I SHOOK my head. "Nix, sister. Maenzer's scared by that phantom picture of his wife that keeps bobbing up in his movie rushes. But he doesn't act like a killer. And he wouldn't have phoned to me to go to his house if he'd been expecting to bump Barkis almost in front of my eyes." I took her wrists. "Carlotta," I said, "you've been feeding me a lot of hooey to steer suspicion away from yourself. You're the one that shot Barkis!"

"No—no!" she wailed. "Take a look at the revolver you took away from me. You'll find only two shots fired out of it. One was the shot I tried to put through your windshield. The second is the bullet I fired at you when you were in Maenzer's den, just after he'd finished running that reel of film through his projector."

I said: "Oh! So you admit firing those two shots, do you?"

"Y-yes. I w-wanted to scare you away. I didn't want you to take Maenzer's case."

"Why not?"

"Because that phantom picture of Vesta on Maenzer's rushes ... it's part of a plan that Barry and I cooked up. We were trying to frighten Maenzer into confessing that he killed Vesta. Maenzer's a spiritualistic believer. We thought we'd be able to make him think Vesta was coming back to haunt him. N-now do you understand?"

Something clicked inside my bean. I said: "Yeah. I'm beginning to understand plenty. And I want you to go home to your apartment right now. Don't leave until I phone you. I'll lend you a topcoat to cover yourself. Take a taxi—and get going right now."

She gave me a funny look. "Wh-what do you plan to do?"

"Trap a killer!" I said. "Now get the hell out."

THE minute she'd gone, I grabbed my phone and dialed police headquarters. I caught my friend, Dave Donaldson of the homicide squad, before he left for the night. "Get up here to my joint right away!" I told him. "I'm going to have a job for you!"

It took him less than fifteen minutes to meet me outside the entrance of my apartment building. I piled into his official sedan and said: "Drive out to Maenzer's house in Beverly—and don't spare the mules!"

"Adolf Maenzer?" Donaldson roared at me. "Say, what the hell are you—a fortune teller or something? We just got a call from Maenzer's place about forty minutes ago. He said a guy named Barkis had been shot at his front door. I've got men out there now, cleaning up and asking questions. How in God's name did you know about it?"

I said: "I was there when Barkis was shot. Now fold up your face and pay attention to your driving."

It didn't take Dave long to get us to Beverly Hills. He braked to a stop in front of Maenzer's house, and we threaded our way past a lot of other official-looking cars until we gained the front door. I rang the bell.

The door opened. I saw Mrs. Hasdorf, the wrinkled little old housekeeper. I said: "We want to see Mr. Maenzer, please."

*"Ja,"* she nodded at me. She led us into the downstairs study, where Maenzer was facing a battery of newspaper reporters.

Maenzer spotted me and drew a sighing sob. "Turner—*Gott sei dank!"* he whispered. "I need your help more than ever. . .!"

I said: "Yeah. But before anything else, I want to go upstairs and take another look at the window that girl climbed out of." To Donaldson I said: "Wait here for me, Dave."

I legged it up to the second floor. But I didn't go near the open window where Carlotta Cordova had climbed down the trellis. Instead, I snapped on my flashlight and found a closet. I looked inside; saw what I'd hoped to find—a tin trunk with wooden slats. I pried it open, started rummaging around. Just as I finished with the photograph album I'd suspected of being here—

*Blooie!* Something bounced down on the back of my skull with the force of a trip-hammer. I pitched forward, buried my schnozzle in the trunk. I wasn't out for more than three or four seconds; but when I got back on my feet, the photograph album was gone and there was nobody in the room with me.

I STAGGERED back into the upper hallway—and saw Maenzer standing at the head of the stairs with an odd look on his pan. "I was beginning to worry about you, Turner," he said.

I said: "I'm okay. Come on downstairs." We went down together, and I buttonholed Donaldson. I said: "Dave, I think I've got your case solved for you. The person who bumped Barkis tonight is the same person who murdered Vesta Delorme a few months ago!"

Donaldson said: "But Vesta's death was an acci-

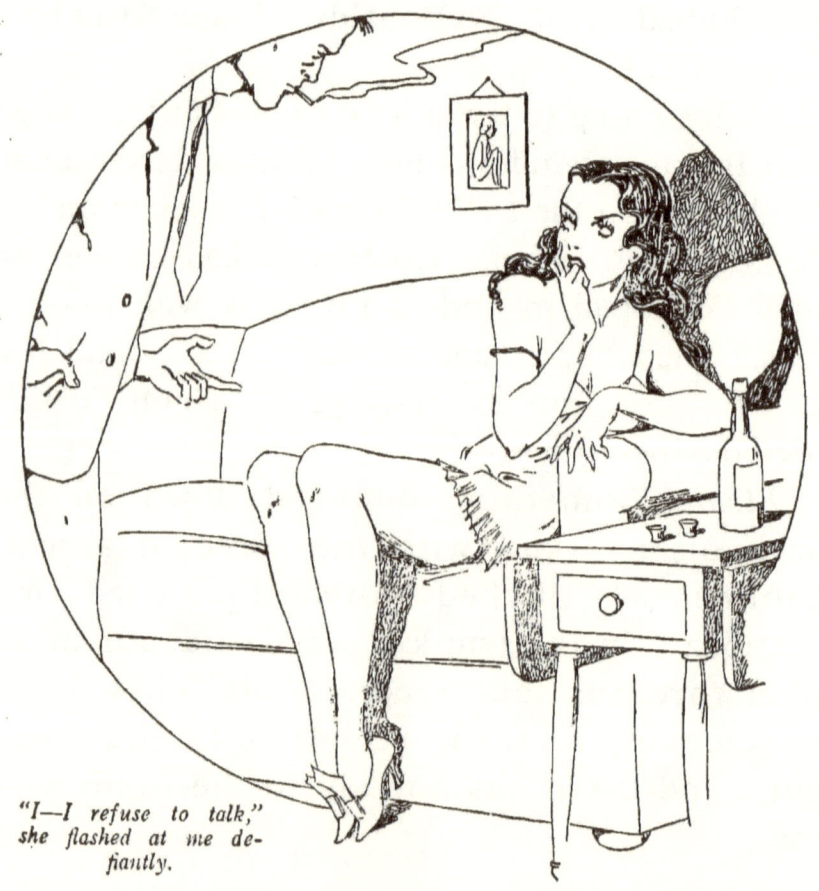

*"I—I refuse to talk," she flashed at me defiantly.*

dent!"

"No. It was murder. The killer tossed a connected electric heater into Vesta's tub while she was bathing."

Maenzer was white. "But—but who—"

I looked him square in the eye and said: "I don't know for sure. But in thirty minutes I'll tell you the murderer's name—just as soon as I've had a chance to ask Carlotta Cordova one question!" Then I turned to Donaldson. "Come on, Dave. I want you to take me downtown to pick up a certain bit of evidence; then we'll get the Cordova cutie!"

Dave and I leaped out of the house; scrambled into his official car. We headed in Wilshire, hell-for-leather. Two blocks beyond LaBrea I said: "Okay, Dave—slow down. Here's the Gaylaird Hotel where Carlotta lives."

"But you said you wanted to go downtown first to pick up a certain bit of evidence."

"That was a stall. Come along." I led him into the Gaylaird, and we went up to the penthouse on the roof of the left turret, where Carlotta had her sumptuous quarters. I rang the bell, and a Chink maid opened the door. I shoved my automatic into the slant-eyed baby's face and said: "Don't make a sound or you'll be shaking hands with Confucius!"

The maid went pale under her yellow skin. I backed her into a corner and said: "Where's Miss Cordova?"

"In—bed, sir."

Ij turned to Donaldson. "Guard Miss Asia, here, while I go boudoir-delving." Then I made a bee-line for the rear of the apartment. I saw a door and opened it. I smelled expensive perfume; and in the room's dim light I saw Carlotta lying in bed, sleeping. One shoulder-strap of her pajama was down half way to her elbow, baring most of a delicious little breast. But I didn't have any time for such things. I saw a French window being slowly opened on the other side of the room; an automatic's muzzle poked in and aimed at the Cordova cutie's heart—

I JUMPED; landed square on top of Carlotta, knocked her out of bed. I went rolling over the floor after her just as that gun in the window went *"Chow-chow!"* Then I was on my feet. I smashed myself at the window, landed outside on the turret-roof terrace. I saw a running figure. I smashed into it.

*"Gott verdammte!"* my captive yelled in an insane whimper. Donaldson came charging toward me, flashing his heavy-duty electric torch. He sprayed light on my prisoner's face. He said: "God in heaven—it's Mrs. Hasdorf! Maenzer's housekeeper!"

I said: "Not just his housekeeper. *His mother, too!*"

The little, wrinkled old woman squirmed under me. *"Ja! His mutter!* He vas ashamed of me because I vas Cherman—because I could not goot English speak. But how did you guess?"

I said: "I found it out when I looked through your trunk in that upstairs room of Maenzer's house. From the way you'd acted, I had an idea you were more than just a housekeeper. You were too interested in Maenzer; no servant would take such good care of him. I went through your trunk, found an old photograph album. I saw pictures of you as a young woman, holding a baby in your arms. And other pictures of that baby as it grew to boyhood, manhood.

"The child was Adolph Maenzer. And there was one photograph of you yourself—autographed 'To my son, Adolf.' That was the tip-off. But just as I found the picture, you sneaked in behind me and biffed me on the head."

"You—you suspected me?" the old lady gasped.

I said: "Sure. I had most of the details figured out; but I had to trap you to prove my case. I realized that your son had been pretty much of a rat. He abused his wife, Vesta Delorme. And he forced you, his mother, to the status of a servant. You allowed that; but Vesta kicked over the traces. She took a lover—Barry Barkis—to get even.

"Then you discovered that Vesta was playing around. Being still loyal to your son, you killed his unfaithful wife by dropping a hooked-up electric heater into her tub while she was taking a bath. That's the truth, isn't it, Mrs. Hasdorf?"

The old lady said: "*Ja. Und* I vould do it again—!"

I set fire to a gasper and said: "Well, you got away with it for a while. The coroner called Vesta's death accidental, and you thought you were safe. But meanwhile, things began to happen. Carlotta, who had been Vesta's friend, got the idea that your son had murdered Vesta. So Carlotta cooked up the double-exposure scheme on your son's movie 'rushes'—made it appear as if Vesta's ghost was haunting the film. She did it with an old Vesta Delorme reel. And your son, being innocent, called me in to break the 'haunt.'

"Then, tonight, Barry Barkis showed up at your son's house. You recognized him as the man who had been Vesta's lover. So you shot him with the very gun you've got in your hand now!"

"*Ja.* He had despoiled my son's home. I killed him the virst chance I got!"

I nodded. "That's the way I figured it. But I had to pin it on you. So in your hearing I mentioned Carlotta as the key to the mystery. That made you scared of Carlotta. You realized she must be the one who was wrecking your son's movie; and you thought maybe she might spill something to incriminate you. Not knowing how much she knew, you determined to come here and kill her to keep her from talking. Isn't that right?"

"*Ja.* But you said you vas going downtown virst. I thought I vould have time—"

I said: "Sure. That's what I intended for you to

think. You did as I expected—and now you'll spend the rest of your life in jail ... unless they decide to hang you."

*"Nein!"* she screamed. Then, suddenly, she squirmed out of my grasp, ran to the parapet. Before I could stop her, she leaped far out into space; went hurtling downward. I heard her scream—just once. After that there was nothing but silence.

Dave Donaldson turned away. He coughed in his throat. I felt a little funny myself. I went back into Carlotta's boudoir—and after Donaldson left, I stayed around a while with Carlotta to get my mind off what had happened.

Carlotta managed to make me forget, after a while.

# MURDER FOR METROVOX

The movie company stood to make a cool million if Stella LaValle died. And the girl did die—in a messy way! It's Dan Turner's job to unravel the riddle, and there are two girls who could help him.

IT was after midnight, and I was as drunk as a fiddler's witch.

So was Ben Crofton, alongside me; but he wasn't too boiled to tool his expensive Hispano roadster along at a merry clip.

Ben had good reason to hit the bottle. As president of Metrovox Studios, he was up to his ventricles in grief.

To begin with, Sally Lorton, one of his most promising young starlets, had disappeared the day before. That's why I was in the picture. Ben was hiring me to find her.

But on top of the Lorton cutie's vanishing act, Metrovox Studios were just about bankrupt. In another few days the sheriff would be padlocking the place. Then Ben Crofton would be out on his neck—unless something altered the situation.

".... uch as somebody bumping off Stella LaValle," he hiccupped to me as he whooshed the Hispano around a corner into Wilshire.

Of course that was just drunken talk, but I was fried enough to string along. I said: "Why Stella

LaValle? I thought you and she were room-mates. Besides, she's your biggest star."

Ben said: "Room-mates, hell! I ditched that part of it some time ago. Besides, her latest two pix didn't even draw ants."

"So you'd like to see her croaked, huh?" I said jocularly. "Then you wouldn't be saddled with her

*"No, I'm not screwy,"
I said. And in two
seconds Donaldson
had her handcuffed.*

whopping salary."

Ben said: "More than that. Turner. If Stella kicked the bucket, Metrovox would collect a cool million of her life insurance. It would pull us out of the hole." Then he grinned and added: "Of course I'm only fooling."

Just then we passed a tall apartment building. It was the stash where Stella LaValle had a whole upper floor for living quarters. There was a dark alley alongside, and I got an idea. I said: "Stop a minute, Ben, I gotta see a man about a dog."

He slapped on his brakes. I got out of the Hispano, walked into the alley. My foot slipped into something soft and yielding.

I said: "What the hell—!" and yanked out my pencil flashlight. I snapped it on. Then I felt a little sick, and I suddenly wasn't swacked any more.

I TURNED, ran to the parked Hispano. I said: "Holy smoke, Ben—you got your wish!"

"Got my wish?"

I said: *"Yeah. Stella LaValle's in that alley, all smashed to hellangone. She's dead as day before yesterday!"*

He got sober damned quick. He popped out of his car, grabbed my arm. "My God, Dan—you're joking!"

"Am I?" I hauled him to the alley, sprayed my flash.

Crofton let loose a moaning urp from somewhere near his insteps. He said: "That's not . . . oh, God! It is! *It's Stella!*"

She wasn't very pretty to look at. She was naked except for thin chiffon stepins and a wisp of a brassiere. She must have fallen a hell of a long distance. When she'd hit the alley's cement paving, parts of her had splattered all over. It was a spewy mess. The lower half of her face was all caved in, and her jet-black eyes were wide, staring. Her white skin, where there wasn't blood on it, gleamed in my flash-glow. So did her long, famous silver-blonde hair. She was wearing fancy step-ins with S. LaV. embroidered in chip diamonds. At a thousand bucks per copy, Stella LaValle's step-ins had made plenty of publicity in the past.

Ben Crofton hung to my arm. "Dan—this is awful!"

I said: "Yeah. Plenty." I pulled him out of the alley, into the apartment-building. I shoved him into the elevator and said: "Fourteenth!" to the operator.

Up on the fourteenth floor I hammered hell out of Stella LaValle's door. Pretty soon it opened. A dame stared out at me.

She was a Filipino, sort of taller than the average. Her nostrils were flat and wide, but she was pretty just the same. Her skin was the color of coffee with a lot of cream in it. I could almost see through her thin pajamas.

I said: "Who are you, sister?"

She didn't have any accent. She said: "I—I am Rosita. Miss LaValle's personal maid." Her grey eyes widened. "What do you want?"

I palmed my private detective's tin and shoved past her. I made a bee-line for Stella LaValle's boudoir, walked in. I saw an open window. It was directly over the alley. I looked outward, downward.

Ben Crofton said: "You—you think she fell out accidentally?"

"Maybe," I told him. I picked up the phone, dialed police headquarters. Meanwhile, Rosita, the Filipino wren, took one gander out the window. Then she let out a yipping bleat. *"Madre de Dios!* Miss LaValle—Miss LaValle—!"

I PUT my hand on her shoulder, shoved her into an overstuffed chair. Then into the phone I said: "Give me Dave Donaldson, homicide squad."

"He's off duty tonight."

I said: "Nuts!" and dialed Dave at his home. I got him. "Dave, this is Dan Turner. Stella LaValle, the movie star, is dead. She either fell or was pushed out her boudoir window. You'd better bring a meatwagon and come look things over." I hung up before he could answer me.

Over on a chair, Ben Crofton was moaning: "Stella! Oh, my God! Stella!"

I said: "Shut up. After all, you net a million fish out of her insurance. That's a lot of geetus. It'll save Metrovox from going under."

He stared at me. "Good God! You talk of money at a time like this...!"

I said: "Sure. After all, you're hiring me to find that cutie who disappeared—Sally Lorton. Now you'll be able to pay me the five grand fee in case I find her."

"To hell with Sally Lorton!" Ben whispered harshly. "Don't you realize Stella LaValle is lying downstairs, dead....?" He seemed pretty busted up.

I looked away from him, put the focus on the Filipino maid. She interested me. She had nice legs and slim hips, and I could see the curve of her breast through the silk of her pajamas. I said: "Well, Rosita—what do you know about all this? Did you hear Miss LaValle scream or anything when she fell?"

"No—no! I was asleep in my room! I heard nothing!" She ran nervous tan fingers through her black hair.

IN a few minutes Dave Donaldson bounced in. I pulled him to one side and said: "Dave, I've got a hunch this is murder."

He said: "Good lord, Dan! Who—?"

I said: "Well, Ben Crofton stands to gain a million bucks through the LaValle dame's death."

"You think he—?"

I shook my head. "No. He was with me all evening, lapping up Scotch."

"Then what in the hell—?"

I said: "Take it easy. Listen. Do me a favor. Throw a scare into that Gugu maid. Pretend you're going to hold her. You can even go so far as to accuse her of tossing Stella LaValle out the window. Frighten the hell out of her—and keep her here until I get back. I won't be gone long."

Dave went over, grabbed Rosita's arms. "Why did

you kill your mistress?" he snarled at her.

I didn't wait to hear her squealing denial. I went downstairs to the lobby, picked up a phone. I dialed

*She was a mess, all right, and I recognized the step-ins.*

the number of a guy I knew: Fritz Cranston. He made sizzling shorts for the stag-smoker and South American trade.

I said: "Fritz, this is Dan Turner. Listen. A few years ago, didn't you make a couple of hot reels with a Filipino wren named Rosita doing the leads?"

"Sure. She danced a hula for me in her birthday

suit. Good-looking baby, for a Gugu. Swell stems and a figure that'd knock your eye out."

"What became of her?"

"She quit the racket, went to work for Stella LaValle as a maid. Why?"

I said: "Look. Do me a favor. Dig out one of those reels for me. I'll be by your place after a while so you can run it off in your projector. I want to see something."

"You bet, Turner. I'll be waiting for you."

I rang off, went back up to the fourteenth floor. I walked into Stella LaValle's apartment, tipped Donaldson the wink. He was still pouring the business to Rosita; but he quit when I signaled him.

I pulled him out into the hall and said: "Listen. Lay off that Filipino wren now. Take a run-out powder. Get your men out of here. Ben Crofton, too. Leave me here alone with Rosita. I want to talk to her. After a while, I'll leave her here. I want you to post a man downstairs; and if Rosita leaves after I do, have her tailed. Find out where she goes. Got me?"

Dave said: "Sure. But I wish to God you'd tell me what's on your mind."

"Five thousand bucks," I said. I turned away from him.

WHEN Dave and Ben Crofton and others had lammed, I went into the boudoir where Rosita was, I said: "Baby you're in a jam."

"Why—why should I be in a jam?" she wanted to know. Her grey eyes looked troubled.

"Because you're liable to be pinched for croaking Stella LaValle, that's why," I told her. "After all, you were the only one in here with her at the time she went out the window."

"But—but I know nothing! I was asleep—!"

"Sure. I know. But try and make the flatfeet believe that."

She said: "Wh-what am I going to do?"

"Well," I looked her over carefully, "maybe I might help you. I'm not a regular shamus. I'm a private dick. My name's Dan Turner."

"B-but I have no money to pay you, Mr. Turner

I said: "Maybe I don't want money." I put a hand on her shoulder, pulled her toward me.

She understood. She was a wise baby. And she was falling for my line of blarney. I was glad of that, because there were certain things I wanted to find out about her. For one thing, I wanted to see better what she looked like beneath the pajamas.

I put my palm under her chin and tilted it. Then I aimed my kisser for her lips. She didn't back away. She parted her lips and gave me everything.

That did things to me. Things I wasn't expecting. I'd started out in a perfectly calm way, but my ideas got sidetracked when she pressed up against me. She started clinging, and that always drives me uts-nay.

After all, I'm human. What the hell?

Maybe ten minutes later, she was straightening her pajama jacket. By that time I knew what I was doing, and I took a good gander at the way she was built.

Then I said: "Kiddo, you're okay. I'm going to help you out from under this rap." I blew her a kiss and walked out.

Downstairs, I spotted the plainclothes bull that Donaldson had planted at the entrance. I said to him: "Be sure and keep an eye peeled. If that Filipino doll comes out, don't lose her."

"Right, Mr. Turner."

I hailed a night-owl Yellow, gave Fritz Cranston's address. Ten minutes later Cranston was leading me into his living-room. He had a portable movie-projector all set up.

"This is the first film I made of the Rosita wren," he said. He started the machinery going, snapped off the room lights.

On the minature screen a chocolate-colored, luscious bit of feminine fluff appeared. She started peeling off her duds. First she wiggled her dress off over her head. Then she smirked for a minute into the camera-lens, her dark eyes challenging. Next her hands fluttered toward her tight brassiere. She went through all the strip-tease motions.

Finally the brassiere came loose. She let it flutter from her fingers. Then she broke into an honest-togosh hooch dance. I got a kick out of watching it, even if it was only on celluloid.

When she got through shimmying, I could see she knew her stuff like nobody's business. I didn't wait to watch her kick off any more duds.

I said: "Okay, Fritz. I've seen plenty. Thanks."

He said: "But wait a minute, Turner, there's some more! You'll see an act here that'll curl your toe-nails."

"Some other time, thanks," I said. I went out, got into the taxi which had waited for me. I'd found out a lot of things, but most of them didn't quite make sense—yet.


THE night-owl Yellow ferried me back to Wilshire. I got out in front of the apartment where Stella LaValle had lived. I saw the plainsclothes copper still standing at the entrance.

I said: "Did the Gugu cutie come out?"

"No. Nobody's left while you were gone—except a red-haired dame with plenty on the ball."

"Okay." I went inside, elevatored myself to the fourteenth. I knocked on the LaValle door.

Nobody answered.

I whispered: "What the hell!" and a premonition hit me. I backed off, hunched my shoulders, batted myself at the door. It gave way. I went stumbling into the living-room.

Something went: *"Blam!"* and a hot slug zizzed

past my left ear. I ducked, hit the floor with my pan. I tried to yank out the .32 automatic I always carry in a shoulder-holster. But I wasn't in position. There came another *"Blam!"* from the boudoir door. A bullet hit the floor, must have struck a knot in the wood. It ricochetted, creased me on the noggin. I saw a billion Neon lights; then I didn't see anything. I was out.

WHEN I got my brains unscrambled, the lights were out. I staggered to my dogs, found the switch, clicked it. I looked around; didn't see anybody. I walked woozily to a sideboard, found a bottle of Vat 69. I let about a pint of it cascade down my throat, and after that I felt better. I set fire to a gasper, went into the boudoir.

I saw a hat on the floor.

I picked it up. The initials "B.C." were inside. I recognized the head-piece. It belonged to Ben Crofton. He'd been wearing it tonight, while we were out gargling Scotch.

But I couldn't be sure whether he'd left his hat here in the boudoir earlier, when he and I first came into the apartment together, or whether he'd accidentally dropped it more recently. If the last were true, then Ben was the bird who had tossed two lead love-tokens in my direction.

Whoever had done the shooting, he'd lammed now. I searched the whole damned apartment—

fourteen rooms and three baths—but didn't find a trace of the trigger-guy. But when I walked into the Gugu maid's room, I found something else—

I found her carcass stretched out on the floor.

She had been knifed. The chiv was still sticking out of her left breast. The pajamas had been ripped half off her. Her brown eyes were wide open, staring at the ceiling—without seeing it.

I said: "Good God!" and looked her over. There were bruises on her upper body; and on her shoulders and arms, too.

Her flesh was cold when I felt it. Her arms and legs were stiffened. She'd never do any more unpeeled hula-dances before anybody's movie camera.

I grabbed for the phone, called police headquarters. Donaldson was there, waiting for some word from me. He said: "What have you found out, Dan?"

"Plenty," I told him. "Rosita, Stella LaValle's Filipino maid, has been knocked off colder than a cucumber. Her corpse is up here in the LaValle apartment with a chiv sticking out of it. You'd better send the meat-wagon out on another trip."

Dave gasped: "I'll be damned! You wait there for me!"

I said: "Nix, pal. I've got work to do. Somebody took a couple of pot shots at me when I came in here. I can see I'm going to earn my five grand."

"What five grand?"

"I'll tell you later," I said. I hung up.

THINGS were beginning to mesh in my mental cog-wheels now. I went into the front room, killed off what was left of that bottle of Vat 69. My head was still buzzing where that ricochetting slug had car-omed off me, and when I looked in a mirror I saw blood on my face. I went to the nearest bathroom, washed it off. Then I stuck a match-flame against a fresh gasper and went downstairs to the street.

I had a taxi drive me around to my own apart-ment so I could get out my own coupe. Driving my jalopy is cheaper than paying out dough to cab-drivers, the way I figure. And I'm all for saving the old geetus. I'm trying to accumulate a retirement fund and get out of this racket before somebody bores a hole in me with a mushroomed slug.

I slid in under my wheel, stepped on the starter. Then I headed for a bungalow court just off LaBrea. It was where Sally Lorton, Ben Crofton's missing red-haired starlet lived. Or rather, where she'd lived before she disappeared the day before.

I walked up to the door of her bungalow and rang the bell. The cutie who had shared the house with Sally Lorton let me in. Her name was Madge Bond.

She was a tall, willowy brunette with plenty of hills and valleys in the proper spots. All she had on when she opened the door was a peach-colored satin nightgown. It clung plenty tight.

She said: "Oh. You again."

"Yeah," I told her. "Busy?"

She flushed. "Certainly not. That is, I'm just busy sleeping. What do you want?"

"I want to come in. I want to ask you some questions about Sally Lorton."

"You asked all the questions in the dictionary today. What more is there?"

I followed her into her living-room and squatted on the divan. I offered her a gasper, took one myself. I said: "Honey, I don't think you shot straight with me today when I questioned you about Sally Lorton."

She got huffy. "What do you mean, I didn't shoot straight with you? Are you insinuating I'm a liar?"

"No, of course not. But maybe you were just covering up for her a little; trying to save her rep."

"Her rep's A-number-one, wise guy."

"How about yours?" I grinned at her. I grabbed her wrist and pulled her down alongside me; put my arm around her.

SHE raised her palm, cracked me across the cheek. "Keep your damn' paws to yourself!"

I said: "Okay, okay. Have it your way. Only I want you to come clean when I ask you one question."

Her eyes flashed. "I'll come clean, all right. But you can't get anything out of me by pawing around. I know the way you work on girls to get them to talk.

I've heard of your methods."

I shrugged and said: "All right. Let it lay. What I want to know is this: Was Sally Lorton intimate with Ben Crofton? Is that how-come he was pushing her up the ladder toward stardom?"

"No. I told you once. Sally Lorton's straight as a string."

"Sure. I know you told me that. But maybe you made a mistake."

"I don't make mistakes about my friends!" she said. She was superior as hell.

I got up. "Which is Sally's bedroom?"

Madge Bond got sort of pale around the gills. Her eyes went to a closed door—which told me what I wanted to know. Then she sprang at me. "You can't go in there! It isn't necessary! You don't have to snoop around—"

"Go to hell, baby," I said. I gave her a shove and went into the missing Sally Lorton's room. I made for a clothes-closet, opened it. I rummaged around until I found a pair of masculine pajamas with "B. C." stitched on the jacket pocket.

I went back out to Madge Bond. "If Sally wasn't on boudoir terms with Ben Crofton, how does it happen his pajamas are in here?"

"You're a liar. Those aren't Ben Crofton's pajamas."

I got sore. I made a grab for her, bounced her on the divan. The low-cut front of her nightgown ripped half open, and gave me a tantalyzing glimpse of creamy flesh. Then I dragged the cigarette out of my kisser.

I said: "Kiddo, unless you kick through with the truth, I'm going to burn my initials into that nice soft skin of yours!"

She tried to fight me off, but I was too much for her. After all, I'm six feet two and I tip the beam at two hundred even. She didn't have a chance.

She started to moan. "D-don't b-burn me!"

I said: "Okay, then. Spill the patter: What about Sally Lorton and Ben Crofton?"

"Y-yes! They were ... intimate ... He ditched Stella for her...."

I said: "So! Then Sally and the LaValle dame were rivals for Ben's affections, huh?" Then I whispered: "A red-haired wren came out of the LaValle apartment building tonight while I was gone, according to the plainclothes shamus. And Sally Lorton is red-headed . . .!"

Madge stared at me. "Wh-what are you talking about?"

"I think I know where Sally is!" I told her. I got up, put on my hat. "So-long, sweetie. Next time be nice to me and I won't play so rough." I went out.

I piled into my jalopy, drove hell-for-leather to the nearest all-night lunch-counter. I grabbed the public phone, slipped a buffalo into the slot, dialed Dave Donaldson.

"Listen, Dave!" I said. "Meet me in five minutes."
I told him where I was. "I think I'm going to hand
you the murderer of that Filipino wren."

He said: "Hot damn! Is it the same one that tossed
Stella LaValle out the window?"

"The same," I told him. "Take the lead out of
your ears. I'm waiting. We may be too late even
now."

I WENT out, stood on the corner. In five minutes,
Donaldson screeched up in his official sedan. He
tore off five dollars' worth of tax-payers' rubber
from his tires, slapping on his brakes. I bounced in
alongside him. I said:

"Out to Ben Crofton's place in Beverly. Get
heavy-footed, son."

"Jeest!" he said, slapping into second and juicing
his motor. "Then it was Ben Crofton who—"

I didn't answer him. I was too busy hanging onto
the doorhandle while he whizzed his jalopy up to 78
by the speedometer.

As soon as I got settled, I said, "Dave, this is a long
hunch I'm playing. I don't want any wise-cracks out
of your kisser in case I'm wrong."

He said: "Go to hell, you big ape.

We hit a winding road leading up to the hills back
of Beverly, where Crofton's big Spanish-stucco
house was located. I reached forward, snapped off
Donaldson's headlights. "Take it slow," I told him.

"Kill your motor and coast the rest of the way."

He did. We parked a little way this side of Crofton's house. I got out; pulled Donaldson with me. "No noise!" I whispered. "And get your roscoe ready."

*I took a good gander and I saw things!*

He nodded. We tiptoed up to the house. It was all dark except for one light burning in a window upstairs on the second floor.

I tried the front door. It was locked, of course. I looked up; saw two silhouettes on the lighted window-shade of that one window. A man's and a woman's.

I fished in my pocket, got out the chain of master-keys I always carry in case of emergency. I tried several. One worked. The front door opened.

"Quiet now!" I whispered to Donaldson. We went inside. I found the stairway. We started up. At the head of the stairs there was a square hall. I saw light trickling around the edges of a door. I crept toward it, with Donaldson at my heels. We listened—

Ben Crofton's voice was saying: "But good God, baby! You don't mean you—"

"Yes! Yes, Ben! I did it! I killed her; and I killed Rosita, the maid. I did it for you, darling. Now you'll never think of her again. She won't have you. You're mine—all mine! Stella ís dead. You'll collect her insurance. You'll keep control of Metrovox Studios. And we'll be together....!"

I bashed myself at the door, thumped it open. Ben Crofton and a red-haired cutie sprang apart. I yelled: "Grab her, Dave! You heard what she said! She confessed both murders! Now get her—quick! *That's Stella LaValle!*"

Donaldson moved like an overfed bear; but he

was fast on his feet just the same. In two seconds he had Stella handcuffed; had her pinioned against the wall. But he had a funny expression on his pan. He was saying: "Stella La Valle. . . .? You must be screwy, Turner! Stella LaValle was killed! She was tossed out her apartment window...!"

I said: "No, I'm not screwy. I'll go over the whole thing for you. In the first place, Stella loved Ben Crofton. She was his biggest star, before her box-office started falling off. Also, she was the girl-friend. But they quarreled, and he ditched her. He took up with a younger girl named Sally Lorton."

Crofton stared at me. His mush was sort of pasty-white.

I went on: "Stella LaValle brooded. She decided to do something about it. She wanted Sally out of the way. She wanted Ben back. And she thought of a way she might win him back to her. A financial way."

"Financial way?" Donaldson choked.

"Sure. By fixing it so he'd get a million bucks and save his studio from bankruptcy."

Dave said: "Jeest!"

"Well," I said, "the first thing Stella did was ab-duct Sally Lorton, her rival. She killed the Lorton girl—which explains her disappearance.

"Then Stella started working on Sally's corpse. She dyed the dead girl's red hair to a silvery-platinum blonde, matching her own. She hid the corpse somewhere in her apartment up there on the fourteenth floor, waiting for nightfall tonight.

"Her next move was to stick a chiv into the ribs of Rosita, her Filipino maid. That made a second corpse she had to hide.

"Then, tonight, she dressed Sally's blondined cadaver in a pair of her own diamond-embroidered step-ins and threw the corpse out her boudoir window. The fourteen-story fall smashed the murdered girl's features beyond hope of identification; but the platinum hair and diamond-studded step-ins were enough to establish the corpse's identity as Stella LaValle. At least, that's the way Stella figured. And in that way, Stella's insurance would go to Metrovox even though she herself was really still alive. Catch on?"

DAVE nodded, looking sort of dumb.

"Next," I said, "Stella stained herself all over; gave herself a chocolate-colored complexion. She inserted wires in her nostrils to make them wide and flat; and she put on a black wig. Then she was all ready to impersonate the Gugo maid she had killed. You see, such an impersonation would keep anybody from discovering her true identity. It would keep the cops from finding out that she was really Stella LaValle—and still alive. That way, the police would never suspect that the corpse in the alley wasn't the real Stella."

Donaldson just stared at me.

I said: "Well, just about that time, Ben Crofton and I stepped into the mess. We discovered the corpse in the alley. The upper part of the dead girl's face hadn't been smashed; and when Ben saw her coal-black eyes he knew it wasn't really Stella. *Because Stella, being a natural blonde, has light grey eyes!*

"But Ben was a fast thinker. At first he started to yeep that the dead girl wasn't Stella; but he happened to remember that million-buck insurance policy. So he switched his tune; pretended to identify the corpse as that of the LaValle dame. He saw a chance to grab a million clams.

"Then Ben and I went upstairs. Stella LaValle, disguised as a Filipino wren, let us in. I noticed her grey eyes, first thing. That didn't seem right to me. Filipinos have brown eyes, usually. I rigged up an excuse to make love to the disguised dame, so I could get her peeled to the buff. I noticed a few places where the brown stain had sort of smeared; hadn't been applied evenly. *The white skin showed through.*

"Next I had a guy run off a movie for me. A film of the real Rosita. It showed the Gugu cutie having dark eyes. Which proved to me that the Filipino maid in Stella's apartment was a fake; wasn't the real Rosita at all.

"I went back to the apartment to force the truth out of her and unmask her. Somebody shot at me. That somebody was *you*, Ben Crofton!"

Ben sank into a chair. "Y-yes. I—I had gone back there to see if I c-could find Stella. I knew she must still be alive. You batted the door open just as I stumbled over a naked corpse in the maid's room. I got panicky. I was afraid I'd be caught and accused of the killing. I—I shot at you—"

"And missed, except for that ricochetting slug!" I grunted. "Well, anyhow, while I was unconscious you got away. When I came to, I found the real Rosita's body. Her flesh was cold, her limbs stiff. She'd been dead a long time. Hours. That told me plenty. It told me she wasn't the one who had let me make love to her a while before.

"I GOT the whole damned story then. I realized that Stella LaValle had merely dragged Rosita's corpse from its hiding-place, planted it in that room after everybody had left. Then Stella soaked off her chocolate disguise with alcohol, put on a red wig, got dressed and walked out into the night, free as air. The plainclothes guy at the apartment entrance saw her go—and never suspected who she was.

"There was just one more thing I had to find out. I learned it from the missing Sally Lorton's house-mate, Madge Bond. I discovered that Sally had been intimate with Ben; had been the cause of his ditch-ing the LaValle dame.

"It all added up. If the dead girl in the alley wasn't Stella, it had to be Sally! Besides, I remembered that

Sally Lorton had coal-black eyes—same as that corpse in the alley. Therefore, Stella LaValle was loose—with two murders on her conscience.

"What would she be likely to do? I figured she'd come here to Ben Crofton, tell him everything and make him take her back. Disguised, with maybe some facial surgery, she could have married him later—and never been suspected."

Dave Donaldson said: "Damn! And we just got here in time to hear her spill her guts!"

"Yeah," I said. I looked at Ben Crofton. "Well, Ben, I found your missing Sally Lorton for you. She's on a marble slab at the morgue, with bleached platinum hair and a smashed up face. You owe me five grand."

He paid me, later, out of the insurance he collected when they hanged Stella LaValle.

# DEATH FOR A NAME

Dan Turner insists that he is a detective, not a blackmailer. Yet when the dynamite is put under the hood of the car ... he looks for the girl ...

BEN MANNHEIMER was a big shot in Hollywood. He was president of Paralta Pictures. But I'd never had much love for him. So when he pulled up a chair and sat down at my table, I wasn't very cordial.

It was in Sardi's chromium-plated eatery. I was having a midnight sandwich and a snort of Vat 69: Mannheimer said: "Hello, Turner. How's the best private dick in Hollywood?"

He had a proposition on his mind. I could tell it from the furtive way he was acting. I said: "I'm okay, thanks. If you've got anything important on your chest, spill it."

He didn't seem to mind the chill I gave him. He grinned it off. "How would you like to make five grand?" he asked me.

I said: "You must want somebody croaked."

He looked a little startled. "No. Not quite that. I want you to get something on William Snowbring for me. Something I can hold over his head to make him drop that lawsuit against Paralta. Frame him with a skirt, or ..."

I gave him a hard look. "Lawsuit, hell. It's Snowbring's wife you're interested in. Everybody's

*I made a flying leap, tackled her.*

talking about the way you're running around with her. You're trying to frame him into a divorce."

Mannheimer shook his head. "You're wrong, Turner. I'm not playing Snowbring's wife, no matter what people say. But I am worried about that suit."

"No soap, Ben," I cut in. "I'm a detective, not a blackmail artist."

He tried to argue by flashing a wad of geetus un-

der my nose. But I waved him away. Pretty soon he got up and left. To me, the place smelled better when he was gone.

As I finished my Scotch, I thought about Mannheimer's trouble with William Snowbring, the former star. The way things stood, Snowbring had a good chance of nicking Paralta for a million clams ... which would toss Mannheimer into receivership.

This Snowbring ham had been a big name once. But booze had bested him. A few months ago, while on a bender in Mexico, he had married a dance-hall *señorita* named Ysobel Ybarra, a brunette cutie with no talent but lots of ambition. She wanted to get into pictures but Snowbring objected. The newspapers had made plenty of headlines out of their romance.

Then Ben Mannheimer had released a feature production that burlesqued Snowbring's amorous antics in a damned malicious way. Seeing a chance to collect some heavy lettuce, Snowbring was now threatening to sue Paralta Pictures for defamation of character.

Personally, I was hoping the ex-star would collect. That Paralta movie had been plenty raw. Mann- heimer should never have produced it.

I paid my check, walked out of Sardi's. The inter- section of Hollywood and Vine was deserted in the yellow wisps of midnight fog. I had parked my ja- lopy around the corner on Vine. I strolled toward it. Then, suddenly, I said:

"What the hell . . .!" and started to run.

SOME drunken lug was climbing into my coupe, stepping on the starter. A street-light sifted across his once-famous profile. He was William Snowbring, the very guy Ben Mannheimer and I had been discussing. Snowbring was fried to the ears, weaving back and forth behind the wheel.

I yelled: "Hey!" and made a lunge for my run- ning-board. But Snowbring was too quick for me. He gunned the gall-bladder out of my motor. My coupe whooshed away like a red-hot comet.

I swore. Then I noticed another coupe parked just behind the spot where mine had been. It was the same make and model.

I yanked out my flash, sprayed the light on this other jalopy's registration certificate. Just as I expected, it was made out to William Snowbring at an address in Hollywood Heights.

I realized what had happened. Snowbring, being ginned to the whiskers, had mistaken my pile of iron for his own; had driven off in the wrong go-chariot.

Well, if his key worked my car, I figured mine would operate his. I started to crawl behind the steering-wheel. I intended to chase him, make him trade heaps when I caught him.

But before I could step on the starter, things happened.

From an alleyway behind me I heard a yell: high, shrill, rasping. It was a woman's scream of jittery fear.

I whirled. I saw a hard-looking red-haired jane struggling in the arms of a big, tough hombre. He had one hairy paw over her kisser to muffle her noise. With his other hand he was trying to hold her still.

I recognized the guy, although he had never met me. He was Lew Devine, a grafting ten-per-center; a third-grade actor's agent who had once been Ben Mannheimer's partner in the early days of Hollywood.

I didn't know the auburn-haired floozie. But she was putting up a whale of a scrap. As she squirmed in Devine's grasp, the front of her frock got torn open. One breast popped out like a luscious white melon. As an old connoisseur of shemale charms, I'm testifying this baby had something on the ball. Her map wasn't so hot. She had flat nostrils, gold teeth. But her figure was all to the mustard.

She was trying to kick Devine where it would do the most good. Her tight skirt was up above her knees, showing about ten inches of smooth thighs. Her legs were *beaucoup* nifty and then some.

I heard Devine snarling: "Pipe down! Let him blow! You want us to get caught?" His free hand slid forward over her bare shoulder. He grabbed soft white flesh. He squeezed.

By that time I reached the alley. I sailed in. I popped a cargo of knuckles against Devine's smeller. He staggered backward, turned the jane loose.

She was in my way. I swept her aside. By accident my hand touched nude flesh. It was warm, satiny. But I didn't have time to think about that. I plunged past her, met Devine with a poke that should have put him under ether for a week.

He had a chin like the front end of a steam roller. He ate that punch as if it had been tapioca. He came back for an encore.

He swung at me. His fist took me on the shoulder, spun me off-balance. I ducked away from him. The red-haired floozie slid by me, her left breast dancing and swinging out of the torn frock as she ran. She dived at the Snowbring coupe, raised the hood.

"Don't hand me that stuff, sister," I said.

I wondered what the hell she was doing. My attention was away from Lew Devine for an instant.

That was all he needed. He brought out a blackjack, bopped me over the noggin. I saw a million lights. I went down, made a dent in the pavement with my face.

Over the buzzing in my ears I heard Devine say: "For God's sake, come on before he wakes up! He don't know either of us ..." Then I heard running footfalls fading into silence.

AFTER a while I managed to push myself to my gams. I had a knot on the back of my skull the size of a full moon. I had staggered to the mouth of the alley. There was no trace of the gold-toothed frill or the ten-per-center who had tickled me with his blackjack. They were gone.

Then a recollection came to me. I remembered what Devine had said to the girl, just as I was about to climb into Snowbring's coupe: "Pipe down! Let him blow! You want us to get caught?"

Suddenly I got the meaning of his words. I leaped for the parked jalopy, flashed my light on it. The hood had been opened by the flat-nosed cutie. I saw two loose wires.

I traced them back to the driver's seat. I pulled up the cushion. Sure enough, there was a triplet of dynamite sticks attached to a wired detonator.

"Damn!" I whispered. Everything was clear to me now. The dynamite had been connected to the car's ignition system. By stepping on the starter, the circuit would be closed and the fireworks turned loose.

And I had damned near stepped on the starter, blasted myself into the Green Pastures!

The red-haired bimbo had saved my life by yelling. Then, while I had battled Lew Devine, she had yanked the wires apart.

I set fire to a gasper to steady my nerves. I decided I'd better find William Snowbring, warn him that Devine was after his scalp.

I pulled the dynamite from under the seat, made sure there were no other explosives in the coupe.

Then I re-connected the ignition system, slid in behind the wheel. I headed for Snowbring's home in Hollywood Heights.

Twelve minutes later I screeched to a stop in front of his house. I dashed up the steps, rang the bell.

Pretty soon the door opened. A sleepy-looking brunette filly put the drowsy focus on me. She said: "What ees eet you weesh?" with a chili-pepper accent.

For a second I couldn't answer her. I was too busy getting an eyeful of her Latin loveliness. She was wearing a negligee three shades thinner than a cobweb. There was a soft light behind her. I could see almost everything she owned in the way of curves. She possessed plenty.

I mean she had what it takes. Her body was the silhouette of a bachelor's dream. Her hips had just the proper flare. Her thighs lilted into legs that were almost too good to be real. I could see her breasts straining outward through the garment's sheerness, like twin invitations. Her shoulders and throat were creamy enough to eat with a spoon.

Then I got a grip on myself. This was no time for the appreciation of feminine charms. I said: "I want to see Mr. Snowbring right away. *Pronto!*"

The black-haired mamma said: "I am verree sorree. My hosban' ees not at home. I do not know when to expect heem."

*"Where's Devine?" I demanded. "I want him!"*

I STIFFENED. So this was Ysobel Ybarra, the dance-hall *señorita* who had married Snowbring in Mexico while he was plastered! I pinned my lamps on her again. The more I saw of her, the less I blamed Snowbring for falling. Or Ben Mannheimer either, if it was true that Ben was playing her. A dame like that could expectorate in my cuspidor any old afternoon.

Maybe I stared at her too long. She frowned, backed into the house. "You weel have to see my hosban' some other time," she said. She started to close the door in my face.

I said: "Wait a second, sweetness. This is damned important. Somebody tried to cool him off tonight. I think I'll wait for him, warn him."

Her dark eyes opened wide. Dazed fear slid across her beautiful map. "You say—you say some-bodee have try to keel my hosban' . . .?" she gasped. Then, before I knew it, she had me by the arm. She dragged me inside the house. "I theenk I know where to find heem! Eet ees a night-club where he spend moch of hees time. I weel take you there at once!" she panted.

That was a break!

And I had another break coming, too. She still clung to my wrist as she raced upstairs. There was panic in every move she made. She seemed afraid I might leave her. She was trembling to beat hell.

She hauled me into her boudoir. She wriggled out of her negligee, right there in front of me. I got a thump out of what I saw. Her naked legs twinkled as she ran to a closet. She yanked down a dress, slipped it over her head and smoothed it over brassiere and stepins.

It was a swell show while it lasted. Then the frock cascaded down over her like a silken waterfall, hid-ing her breasts, her hips, her thighs ...

She slipped her bare feet into spike-heeled pumps, grabbed up a light coat. "Come queek!" she whispered. She dragged me down a rear stairway, out through a back door. We pelted to a three-car garage behind the terraced yard.

She opened the sliding door, switched on a weak light. She started for a Rolls roadster. Then she tensed. She stared at a coupe in the end stall.

"Eet ees my hosban's coupe! He must have joost come home!" she gasped.

I took one gander at that jalopy. My heart jumped six ways from Sunday. It was my own buzz-buggy; the one Snowbring had driven by mistake!

I said: "For God's sake!" A hunch kicked me in the hip pockets. I hauled open the coupe's door on the driver's side.

My guess was correct. William Snowbring's corpse tumbled smack into my f ace.

I jumped backward. His body hit the garage floor with a squidgy sprawl. His throat had been slashed from ear to ear. Fresh blood was all over him. It was a nasty mess.

I didn't need a dream-book to reconstruct what must have happened. Snowbring must have come straight home after grabbing my coupe by error. And someone had tailed him, croaked him here in his own garage before he could climb out of the car!

Things began to click in my think-tank. I remembered Lew Devine and the gold-toothed dame in that alley behind Sardi's. I had lost a lot of time hauling the dynamite out of Snowbring's coupe before driving out here to Hollywood Heights. In that period, Devine would have had plenty of time to reach Snowbring's garage.

There was one thing in my favor now. Lew Devine didn't know that I had recognized him in Sardi's alley. He had said as much to his red-haired girlfriend as they lammed. Well, the joke was on Devine. I knew his identity.

A SOUND brought me out of my thoughts. It was Snowbring's Spick spouse. She let out a bleating yeep. *"Madre de Dios—!"* she screamed. Then her knees went out from under her.

I caught her as she fell. She was out cold. I said: "Damn it to hell!" and lifted her in my arms. I managed to switch out the garage light, close the sliding door, snap the padlock behind me. Then I carried her back to the main house.

I raced up the rear stairway with her, dumped her on the bed in her rose-lighted boudoir. There was a phone alongside the bed. I snatched it, dialed my friend Dave Donaldson of the homicide squad.

His voice growled: "Hello. Who is it and why?"

I said: "This is Dan Turner. I'm at William Snowbring's house in Hollywood Heights. Snowbring is deader than last Leap Year. Murdered. Yeah. Somebody helped themselves to a slice of his throat. And I think I know who did it."

Donaldson yelped: "For the love of—! Who—"

"I'm not saying anything yet," I snapped back.

"I've got a personal grudge against the guy I suspect. He's a ten-per-center around Hollywood. He almost let me blow myself into a jigsaw puzzle. I want the pleasure of nabbing him personally. You dash out here to Snowbring stash with a stiff-wagon and a medical examiner. I'll phone you if I nail the bozo I'm after. I've got to find out where he lives."

Dave said: "See here! You can't do that! You're not a regular cop! You—"

"Nuts," I told him and hung up.

I took another squint at the Mex dame on the bed. She was still in a dead faint. I didn't have time to toss water in her puss, try to bring her around. I turned, lammed downstairs, piled myself into Snowbring's coupe where I had parked it at the curb.

I headed for Western Avenue.

At Hollywood and Western I dived into an all-night druggery, thumbed a phone-directory. Lew Devine wasn't listed. I looked through the city directory, found the address where he lived. It was an apartment-house just off Sunset. I bought a fresh pack of gaspers. slammed myself back into the coupe and took off.

No traffic-signals were working at that late hour. And I didn't bother with boulevard stops. I made time. Pretty soon I pelted into the building where Devine hung out.

I took the steps three at a time, reached the second floor. I came to his door.

I reached inside my coat, hauled out the .32 automatic I always carry in a shoulder-holster. I pointed it ahead of me and knocked with my left mitt.

For a minute, nothing happened but silence. Then the door opened. I shoved my roscoe forward and said: "Bullets don't taste very good. You want a mouthful, Mr. Devine...?"

The last words stalled on the end of my tongue. And no wonder!

IT WASN'T the ten-per-center who had opened up for me. It was a dame. It was the red-haired, gold-toothed floozie whose yell had saved me from setting off those firecrackers a while before;

Her wide nostrils flattened as she drew a gasping breath of surprise. She opened her kisser. "Y-you...!"

She was wearing peek-a-boo pajamas that didn't hide very much of her these and those. Her hand went to her left breast, mashed it flat against her heart.

I said: "Yeah, me." I shoved her backward, entered the room, closed the door behind me. I kept her covered with my rod. I said: "Where's Devine? I want him."

"He—he isn't here."

"Oh, no? Then where the hell is he?"

"I d-don't know."

I put my palm flat against her face and pushed. I said: "Don't hand me that stuff, sister. Listen. De-

vine's a murderer and you know it. But I won't drag
you into the mess if I can avoid it. I owe you a good
turn. You saved my bacon tonight when you yelled
at me and stopped me from setting off that dynamite in Snowbring's coupe."

She got ivory-pale. "I don't know what you're
talking about!"

I said: "Okay. You're dumb. You don't know the
score. That suits me. Just tell me where to find Lew
Devine. That will let you out. But make it snappy
before I get sore and change the color of your eyes."

"I—I don't know where he is. I haven't seen him
since we ran away and left you in that alley...."

I grinned at her. "So you admit that much, do
you? Well, that ties you up nice and tight, baby. It's a
confession that you had something to do with the
dynamite planted in Snowbring's jalopy. You knew
it was there or you wouldn't have screamed at me,
warned me."

Her shoulders slumped. "All right. You win. I was
in on the dynamite deal. I admit it. But it ain't such a
tough rap for Lew and me, after all. Nobody got
killed."

I said: "The hell it's not a tough rap. It's a hanging
job and you know it. Snowbring is dead. His throat
was cut in his garage a while ago. Add that up on
your fingers, kiddo."

That's where I made a mistake. I shouldn't have
spilled my guts so soon. The red-haired bimbo stiff-

ened. A pulse stood out on her throat. She said: "Snowbring ... dead ...? Then Lew must have followed him and—" Suddenly she closed up like a clam with lockjaw.

I realized I'd put my foot in it. Now she wouldn't tell me where to find her ten-per-center boy-friend. Not when he was facing a murder rap. By telling her Snowbring had been rubbed out, I had put a cork in her kisser.

Something had to be done about it. I holstered my gat, grabbed her around the waist, pinned her arms to her sides. I said: "Either you're going to talk or you'll wish to God you had!"

She squirmed, wriggled, tried to get away from me. Her body was warm and soft through the thin pajamas. It sent my temperature up seven degrees. I said: "Sweetheart, you'd better talk damned fast before I lose control of myself. They tell me I'm hard to handle when that happens."

I slapped her hard across both cheeks, sending her reeling back against the sofa. I hopped after her fast; she expected to get mussed up and cowered away from me. "No! No...!"

I clamped my mouth over her lips, and when I kiss a jane, she stays kissed a hell of a long while. This time was no exception. And I was plenty rough. I fed her everything I knew in the way of technic.

I figured she'd realize what was likely to happen next. Maybe she'd break down and tell me what I wanted to know before I went too far. But she was hardboiled. She could absorb a lot of that kind of punishment. She seemed to like cave-man stuff and before I knew it she was dishing it right back at me, boiling hot!

Right then I forgot my original purpose. I got wrapped up in my work. I poured a dozen more kisses into her; fumbled around until I had her shoulders bare. I stroked her satin-smooth skin until she quivered.

She started to moan. Her mouth pressed against mine, clung there....

AFTER a while she grinned at me. She said: "Well, you're getting nowhere fast, ain't you, Big Shot?"

I said: "Maybe. But I'm not through with you yet. I just went soft on you there for a while. I know some other tricks. You don't know how real tough I can be ... yet!"

"Torture-stuff, eh?" she said. "Well, you needn't bother. I've been thinking things over. I'm going to come clean with you."

I said: "Oh! So you've thought things over, huh?"

She giggled up at me. "You can make a gal think, Handsome." Then she got serious. "Listen; I know when I'm in a spot. And I'm in one now—up to my eyebrows. To hell with Lew Devine. I can't worry about what happens to him. I want to make a deal with you if you're willing."

I said: "What kind of a deal?"

Her eyes narrowed. "A while back, you said you owed me a good turn because I warned you away from that dynamite. You said you'd keep me clear of the mess if I told you where to find Devine."

"Yeah," I said. "And it still goes. Where is he?"

She said: "Look. I'm shooting the works. Lew Devine planted the dynamite in Snowbring's car. I was his lookout while he did it."

"I know that much. Get down to cases."

She said: "Wait. You've accused Devine of cutting Snowbring's throat. I wouldn't know about that. I wasn't with him. After you got conked in the alley behind Sardi's, I came straight home here to Devine's apartment. A little later, he phoned me. He said he'd be home in about an hour." She looked at a clock on the desk at the other side of the room.

*"I never trust dames," I said. I made a loose fist and slugged her.*

"That means he ought to be showing up pretty soon."

I got to my feet. "Are you leveling with me?"

"Sure I'm leveling. I'm trying to save my own skin. You can wait here for Lew. You can trap him. He won't suspect that anybody's here except me. That's where he'll be surprised. I'll be gone."

"Oh, yeah?"

She said: "Yes. I've shot square with you. Now live up to your promise. Turn me loose. Let me lam. Then you can wait here for Devine to show up."

I figured she was telling the truth. But I wasn't taking any chances. I said: "Baby, if you haven't lied to me I'll guarantee to keep your skirts clean. On the other hand, I never trust dames." Then I made a loose fist, hit her on the point of the jaw.

She went out cold.

I LIFTED her, carried her to the bathroom, put her on the floor with a bathrobe under her to keep off the chill. I locked her in. Then I went to the front room, dialed the Snowbring house in Hollywood Heights.

A copper answered the phone. I said: "Is Lieutenant Donaldson still there?"

The cop said: "Yeah." Then, in a minute, Dave got on the wire. He said: "Well?"

"This is Dan Turner. I'm in the apartment of a guy named Lew Devine, on Sunset." I told him the address.

"So what?" he growled.

I said: "So get out here as fast as wheels can bring you. We're setting a trap." Then I hung up before he could ask a lot of unnecessary questions.

I set fire to a gasper, settled down to wait. If everything worked all right and we caught Devine, I intended turning the gold-toothed floozie loose. But if she had fed me a bum steer, I had her where I wanted her. I felt pretty good.

I started pacing the floor. Donaldson was a hell of a long while getting there. Just for practice I decided to go through the drawers of the desk over on the other side of the room. I figured I might find something that would tell me why Lew Devine wanted to murder Snowbring.

There wasn't much in the first drawer except old papers, receipted bills. But in the lower drawer I saw an envelope. I opened it, pulled out a legal-size paper. I said: "What the hell!"

It was an agent's ten-per-cent contract: one of Devine's iron-clad forms. It was all made out, signed, witnessed. I looked at the signatures. I felt as if I'd been slugged in the mush.

Just then somebody knocked at the front door. A voice said: "Open up, Turner. It's Donaldson."

I leaped forward, let him in. He said: "What's this dope about a trap?"

"We're waiting for Lew Devine," I said. "But I just

discovered something that may change my theory. I—"

Dave's eyes had been glancing around the room. Now he interrupted me. He pointed to a closet in a far corner. He said: "What the hell is that trickling from under the door? Looks like blood to me."

I stared.

There was a thickish red fluid seeping out on the floor. It hadn't been there a while ago. My throat got tight. I cursed, rammed myself at the closet, yanked it open.

A propped-up corpse slumped out of the tiny space, landed at my feet with a bouncing thud.

It was Lew Devine. There was a stab-wound over his heart. He was already getting stiff with rigor mortis. Blood had welled down from his chest, finally puddled out under the closet door.

I said: "Damn! I wonder if that red-haired bimbo knew he was in here? Was she horsing me along—?" The words choked against my goozle. I whirled, slammed myself at the locked bathroom door. I wrenched it open.

THE gold-toothed floozie was gone. So was the bathrobe I had placed under her. A window was open. It led to a fire-escape outside.

I saw something tiny, yellow, on the floor. I grabbed it up—and I had the answer to my puzzle.

I clutched Donaldson's arm, hauled him out of

the apartment. "Come on, Dave! We're headed for Ben Mannheimer's house in Beverly!" I panted.

"What for?" he lumbered down the stairs after me.

I said: "Shut up. Don't ask questions. I'll just tell you this much. I found a contract in Lew Devine's desk a minute ago. It was with Mannheimer's Paralta outfit. Let's get started!"

We bounced into Donaldson's official jalopy. I drove; and I didn't spare the carburetor. I souped that bus to eighty-seven; made it to Mannheimer's place in Beverly Hills in twenty minutes flat.

Dave and I sprinted for Mannheimer's front door. I told him to be quiet. I fumbled with the skeleton keys I always carry; found one that worked the lock. We went inside; sneaked up the stairs. I saw a closed bedroom door with light trickling around its edges. Voices carne from inside the room. A dame was saying: "I've got to have your copy of that contract, Ben! I didn't have time to find Devine's copy. But I'll go back and get it later. They've got to be destroyed, I tell you! Otherwise I'll be caught—"

Mannheimer's low-pitched growl broke in. "To hell with you! Beat it. I don't want to be mixed up in this. You shouldn't have come here."

The female voice snapped back hysterically. "Listen! You promised to make me a star when Snowbring was dead. Well, he's dead. I killed him. And I had to kill Devine too, when I learned that damned Turner dick knew his identity. Now you've got to see me through! You talked me into this, and—"

I didn't wait for any more. I smashed into the door with my shoulder, went lunging into the room. Donaldson followed me. I saw Ben Mannheimer in bed. A frill was standing beside him. It was the red-haired, gold-toothed floozie who had escaped from the bathroom in Devine's flat.

She screamed, started for the open window. The bathrobe she was wearing flew out behind. Naked white legs flashed. Then the loose robe tripped her. She stumbled, landed in a heap of flailing limbs and white girl-flesh. I made a flying leap, wrapped my aims around her thrashing thighs, mashed her soft body flat with my weight. I yelled: "Put the nippers on her, Dave! You heard her confession!"

Donaldson leaned over, clicked the cuffs on her wrists. I yanked her upright. From my pocket I pulled the tiny gold object I'd picked off Devine's bathroom floor. It was a thin gold shell made to fit over the front tooth.

I pried the red-haired cutie's mouth open, flicked out the three other gold shells she was wearing. Her real teeth gleamed white, perfect. The contour of her mouth was changed.

She tried to bite my fingers. I whammed her across the kisser. Then I reached up in her nostrils, pulled out the tiny wire shapes that made her nose look flat, widened. Her smeller resumed its natural shape—straight, aquiline.

And last I yanked the red wig from her head. It was fastened pretty tight. I pulled some of her real hair away with it. *Her short black hair.*

I said: "Now you look more natural, Ysobel Ybarra—or rather, *Mrs. William Snowbring!*"

Donaldson stared. He said: "What in God's name...?"

I said: "The whole thing is very simple. Ben Mannheimer, here, was scared of Snowbring on account of that threatened lawsuit. He wanted Snowbring out of the way. He started going around with Mrs. Snowbring; told her he'd make a movie star of her.

"But Snowbring didn't want his wife on the screen. So then Mannheimer told the dame she ought to kill her hubby. Isn't that right, Mannheimer?"

THE Paralta president was green around the fringes. He choked: "Y-yes. But I didn't—"

I said: "No. You didn't have anything to do with the actual murder of Snowbring. His wife took care of that. She had hooked up with an agent, Lew Devine. Devine got her a contract with Paralta. I found it in his desk. Here it is." I flashed the document I had found in the ten-per-center's drawer.

Donaldson looked fuddled. "I still don't see—"

I said: "Mrs. Snowbring wanted her husband out of the road so that she could be a star. The publicity she'd get as the widow of a famous murder-victim would put her over. She persuaded Lew Devine to help her. She disguised herself dropped her phoney accent. She and Devine planted dynamite in Snowbring's jalopy.

"But the scheme didn't jell because Snowbring drove away in the wrong car. Then I came along, started to set off the bomb. Mrs. Snowbring lost her nerve. She yelled, warned me. Then Devine bopped me with a blackjack, left me unconscious. He didn't know I had recognized him. Neither did Mrs. Snowbring."

Ysobel Ybarra-Snowbring spat at me. "You rat!"

I shrugged. "She and Devine trailed Snowbring out to his garage," I continued to Donaldson. "They cut his throat. Then Devine went home to his apartment while Mrs. Snowbring sneaked into her own boudoir, took off her disguise.

"Shortly afterward, I showed up. I didn't recognize Mrs. Snowbring as the red-haired floozie because her make-up had been too perfect. She was startled to see me. She put on an act, let me discover her husband's corpse. Then she pretended to faint. She overheard me phoning headquarters. From what I said over the phone, she realized I had Lew Devine's number: knew I had recognized him. When I left her house, she saw she was in a jam. If I put the collar on Devine he might break down, spill his guts, implicate her.

"So she had to kill him to shut his mouth. She got up, disguised herself again, drove hellity-larrup to Devine's flat. She beat me there because I lost some time looking up his address and buying cigarettes. She knifed Devine, stuffed his body in the closet. She was just starting to look for that contract when I arrived.

"She put on another act for me; fooled me again. And when I locked her in the bathroom, she escaped."

Donaldson said: "But how did you link Mannheimer in the deal? How did you know—"

I set fire to a gasper. "When I found that contract in Devine's desk, I began to catch wise. It was a contract with Paralta Pictures to star Mrs. Snowbring. I remembered how Mannheimer had been playing around with her. Then when we found Devine's corpse I was almost sure of my ground. That false gold tooth on the bathroom floor cinched things. I knew Mrs. Snowbring was the red-haired dame in disguise. And I knew she'd come here to Mannheimer's house, try to get his copy of that contract and destroy it. The contract linked her with her husband's death; supplied the motive. She was hoping she could find Devine's copy later, burn it. But we beat her to it."

Ben Mannheimer bleated: "You've got it exactly

right, Turner! I'll testify to it if it will save me from jail! I—"

I turned away from him, looked at Dave Donaldson. I said: "You clear up the details, Dave. I'm leaving. I still think it smells bad when Mannheimer's around."

# MURDER ON THE SOUND STAGE

One movie murder leads to another, and Dan Turner finds more danger than assistance from the girls in the case!

## CHAPTER I.
### The Lady Comes Clean

I WALKED INTO Jeffery Fenwick's unlighted dressing-bungalow on the Altamount lot, wondering why he had sent for me. It was around eight o'clock at night. I fumbled for a wall-switch.

From the darkness behind me, a hysterical feminine voice shrilled: "Start praying, Mr. Fenwick! I'm going to kill you for what you did to my sister!"

It startled the living hell out of me. I wasn't expecting to find anybody in that bungalow. Jeffery Fenwick himself, the Altamount star, was over on Sound Stage "A." They were shooting some retakes on his latest picture. A little while before, he had phoned me at my apartment, said he wanted to see me about something damned important. He had asked me to come to the studio, wait for him in his dressing-quarters until he was through doing his stuff before the cameras.

Now some goofy frill was getting ready to cool me off, thinking I was Fenwick!

She was rasping: "I'm going to shoot you and say you attacked me! I'll tell the police you tore my dress off, and I had to kill you in self-defense!"

I heard the click of a roscoe's hammer on the

other side of the room. I said: "What the hell!" and dived sidewise, smacked the floor with my smeller. Then I yelled: "Hold everything, you fool! I'm not Fenwick—my name's Dan Turner!"

As I spoke, a light came on. I heard a gasping: "Oh-h-h—my God! It's true! You're not—"

I scrambled to my pins. I blinked.

There was a blonde cutie standing over me. Her costume was what you might call informal. She was

When she yelled, Frizzati came in with his hands high. "Listen, copper—for Gawd's sake—!"

the niftiest wren I ever put the focus on.

She had torn her own dress down the front, half way to her

waist. It hung in tatters from her bare white shoulders. What it revealed of her figure was gorgeous. I've seen plenty of undraped women, but this one had me hanging on the ropes! Through a ripped place in her skirt, I caught a quick gander at ivory skin, rosetted garters.

Her eyes were wide, staring. She was holding a tiny, pearl-handled gat in her mitt. It wavered uncertainly. Her trigger-finger looked itchy.

I leaped at her.

With my left, I twisted the little roscoe out of her hand. Then I splatted my right palm full across her cheek, knocked her staggering. I grabbed her, crushed her in my arms.

She squirmed, struggled, wailed. I could feel the warmth of her against my chest. My blood-pressure went up a notch. I tripped her. She went sprawling to the floor. I smashed her down with my two hundred pounds of weight.

I said: "Okay, baby. It's the Bastille for you!" I flashed my tin in front of her map.

She chocked, went pale. "You—you are a policeman—?"

"Private dick," I clipped back. "And I'm going to toss your pretty little ears into the calaboose for safe-keeping. So you were going to bump Jeffery Fenwick, were you?"

She stared at me defiantly. "Yes!"

"What for?"

"Because he deserves to die—the rat! I'll get him if it takes me a lifetime!"

I said: "Is that nice, baby? Murder's a hanging rap in sunny California. Or didn't you know that?"

SHE wriggled then, tried to get loose. I got a definite slap out of her struggles, she being held in the hold I held her in! She was in her early twenties, at a guess. And she was a knockout.

"Let me go!" she moaned.

I said: "Not yet, sweetness. I want to have a little conference with you. How-come you're gunning for Jeffery Fenwick? What's the large idea?"

"He k-killed my sister!" she whimpered. All of a sudden her eyes puddled up. Her lower lip got tremulous.

I said: "Fenwick killed your sister? Are you trying to tell -me he's a murderer?"

"He's worse than a murderer!" she grated. "He p-promised to marry her, five years ago. Back in Trenton. He was a taxi-driver, in those days. My sister loved him. She loved him...too much! Then he got tired and walked out on her."

I caught wise. "Then what happened?"

"She t-took poison before the baby was born."

I thought that over. I wasn't particularly surprised. It sounded like something the Fenwick ham might have done. I'd never liked him much, even though he was now one of the biggest stars on the screen. In two pix, he had attained top billing, top salary. He was a dark, Latin-looking bozo; and there was something about him that women fell for.

He never talked of his past, even for publicity purposes. Nobody seemed to know where he came from or what he had been before he hit Hollywood. He had been with Altamount Pictures less than a year. In that short space of time, he'd not only become a star, but he'd also married Asta Valenska, the nifty Russian hotsy-totsy who played opposite him. Now it looked as if his past had caught up with him.

I eased up on the blonde cutie. I said: "Now listen to me, sweetness. Maybe Fenwick did everything you claim. If he did, I don't blame you for hating his guts. But murder isn't the answer. You're just inviting a hemp necklace for your pretty throat."

Her eyes blazed deep blue fire. "Five long years I've searched for him! I swore I'd send a bullet through his heart for what he did to my sister. And that's what I'm going to do—some day, somehow! I saw him in a picture a couple of months ago. I recognized him, even though he'd changed his name. So I came to Hollywood to kill him—and nobody's going to stop me!"

I said: "That's what you think, kiddo. But maybe a year in the jug will change your mind. I'm placing you under arrest for attempted assault with a deadly weapon. Come on—get going."

I stood up, pulled her to her feet. She nestled

close. I know lots about women, but she was the cuddliest little honey I ever met!

Of course I hated to think of her behind iron bars. She seemed too young, too wholesome and sweet. But maybe a short stretch would cool her down a little; knock some of the hate out of her heart. It would be better than a hanging rap, I figured.

She looked up at me. "You—you're taking me to j-jail?"

I nodded, trying to make my expression hard.

She jerked her arms free. Then she wrapped them around my neck; pulled my head downward. Her lips parted over mine.

I've been kissed by experts in my day. But I got a new kind of thump out of this one. There aren't many innocent lips in Hollywood; yet that's the way the blonde wren's kiss seemed to me. Innocent—and damned thrilling for that very reason. It was like exploring territory that's never been explored before.

I can't explain it after all, a kiss is a kiss. But there's apparently more to a kiss than just kissing. I could feel her body quivering against me. Her breath was like liquid fire. "I—I don't want to be arrested!" she whispered pleadingly. "Don't s-send me to jail!"

I almost went haywire. After all, I'm human. And she was damned lovely. I fell into a clinch, ran my fingers through her yellow hair. I started to bury my kisser against the hollow of her throat. I was beginning to lose control. I had an awful yen for that dame ...

THEN I got a grip on myself. I'd be a heel to take advantage of her predicament. She was in a jam; and she was trying to bribe me the only way she could. I didn't blame her a damned bit. But I just couldn't see myself getting low enough to go through with such a deal.

I let her loose and she just stood there, her eyes big, her hand to her mouth. "Come on, sweetness." I said quietly. "Pull yourself together."

She swayed on her feet scared again. "You—you're g-going to arrest me, after all?" It was almost a sob.

I shook my head. I said, "I'm going to turn you loose—if you'll promise me to scram out of town and let Jeffery Fenwick alone. How about it? Is it a bargain?"

Two big tears skidded down her cheeks. "I—I—"

"Make up your mind," I said. "Promise me—or go to the hoosegow." Then I grabbed her, shook her until every delicious curve of her body trembled. "Use your noggin, baby. You're too young and pretty to hang. You say your sister is dead. Okay— killing Fenwick won't bring her back to life. Run on back home to Trenton and forget about him. It's just one of those things."

She looked at me. "I—I guess you're right," she whispered. There was a catch in her throat. "You—you'll let me go if I give you my word I won't do anything ... foolish? You w-won't say anything about what just happened?"

I said: "Honor bright. kiddo."

She threw her arms around my neck and she kissed me again. It was different, this time. No emotion—just gratitude. I drew a hell of a large wallop out of it just the same. "You're sweet!" she said.

Then she went over to a corner. picked up a coat. She slid into it; buttoned it to cover her torn dress.

She went out.

I sat down, set fire to a gasper. Now that I was alone, my think-tank began working. It looked to me as if Jeffery Fenwick must have known he was in danger. That's why he had sent for me, most likely.

In fact, I remembered what he had said to me over the phone: "Mr. Turner; I need a good private detective. I'm desperate. You were recommended to me. Can you see me tonight, at the Altamount lot? There's danger involved, but I'll pay you whatever fee you ask—"

There in his dressing-bungalow, I now nodded to myself. He had probably known that the blonde wren was on his trail. He was scared of what she might do to him. Besides, he most likely wanted to find some way of keeping her quiet about his past. A scandal would play hell with his movie career.

He was a louse; no doubt of it. Any man who gets a girl to fall for him like he had and then runs out on her is worse than a louse. I made up my mind to have nothing to do with him. But hell—he wouldn't need my services now. He was out of danger. I had talked the blonde cutie out of her murder-notions; persuaded her to go back east. I had even taken her roscoe away from her—.

I felt in my coat pocket, where I had slipped her gat. Then I leaped to my pins. I said: "What the hell—!"

The gun was gone!

All of a sudden I realized what had happened. The yellow-haired chicken had made a sucker out of me. That last kiss she gave me—that hadn't been gratitude as I had thought. It was a trick. While her lips were against mine, she must have picked my pocket; got her roscoe back!

That spelled trouble. Bad trouble. I felt it in my bones. She wouldn't have wanted her gat back— unless she was still figuring to plug Fenwick!

I said; "Damn it to hell!" and went pelting out of that dressing-bungalow. I'd have to warn Fenwick, much as I despised him. I tore across the lot, reached Sound Stage "A" where he was working—.

Just as I gained the big, soundproof door of the looming stage building, it opened. The overhead red light winked out. The green carne on. Then, from inside, there came the damnedest scream I ever listened to.

## CHAPTER II.
### Death in a Fog

IT RASPED against my ear-drums like a file bit-
ing through tempered steel. It was shrill, high-
pitched, crazy. It made my blood run cold;
brought goose-pimples to my skin the size of canta-
loupes.

I've heard plenty of female shrieks in my day,
drunken and otherwise. But this had a shattering
hysteria that put the chill down my back. There was
terror in it; and a touch of madness, too.

It ended in a choked gurgle.

I snapped out of my trance, went smashing into
the building. I almost did a ground loop over a snake
of electric cable. I recovered myself, sprinted toward
a vast and gloomy set at the far end of the place.

For a minute or two I couldn't see anything. In
spite of the lights, the stage was choked with a thick
grey pall. It was like a cloud of drifting smoke. It ed-
died to my nostrils; smelled and tasted like essence
of wintergreen.

Then I understood what it was. Fake fog—studio
mist. To make it, they spray clear oil out of powerful
nebulizer-nozzles. It drifts and settles just like real
fog. To make it less unpleasant for the people on the
set, they add concentrated wintergreen flavoring to

the oil before they vaporize it.

As I looked forward, I saw a group of grips and juicers operating a queer-looking gadget. It was an electric motor attached to a suction-pump. On the other end of the pump there was a length of thick canvas tubing, like an oversize vacuum-cleaner. In fact, that's what it was: a smoke-eater. The same kind of fume-dispersing equipment that metropolitan fire-departments use.

With the motor whining, the grips carried the canvas tube from one spot to another. It sucked up the fog-mist. In less than three minutes the set was fairly clear. I could see everything, everybody.

The set showed the exterior of a big, ghostly looking, abandoned house. Two movable camera-cranes stood before the set, for angle-shots. A third blimp-encased camera rode on a portable dolly for walking sequences. A fourth was stationary. A trio of microphones dangled from overhead booms.

The first guy I tabbed was Foster Kinkaid, the production's director. He was a friend of mine. He was scrambling down from his chair on one of the two camera-cranes.

I collared him as he reached the floor. "What the hell's up?" I barked.

He said: "Turner! My God—how did you get here?"

"Jeffery Fenwick sent for me," I told him. "He's in danger of some sort."

Kinkaid said: "Danger, hell! *He's dead!* Somebody just shot him!"

I felt as if a mule had kicked me square in the teeth. "Fenwick—croaked—?" I panted.

Kinkaid grabbed me by the arm, jerked me onto the set. My thoughts were all scrambled to hellangone. So the blonde baby had beaten me to the sound stage! She had carried out her threat! She had put a slug through Jeffery Fenwick!

I SPOTTED a slim, sinuous brunette crouched over an outsprawled form. Her black dress clung to her snaky figure like a coat of enamel. She had more curves than a scenic railway. I recognized her. She was Asta Valenska, the Russian star. She was leaning over the corpse of her murdered husband, Jeffery Fenwick.

Fenwick himself was stretched out on his back. He still looked handsome, even in death. He'd had what it takes to drive dames dippy. I'll say that much for him. But his Casanova days were over, now. You can't make love with a bullet through your skull and your brains oozing out over your left ear.

Foster Kinkaid groaned: "It's awful! We were shooting the last scene of the new Fenwick-Valenska pic. Fog stuff. There was to be gun-play. At the correct moment, a shot was fired. Then Asta—Miss Valenska—screamed."

I said: "Yeah. I heard her."

"I didn't kill him, Mr. Turner —I didn't. . . ! You've got to believe me, because you're the only one who can help me!"

Kinkaid said: "But her scream wasn't in the script. In the play, she was supposed to be Fenwick's enemy.

She wanted him killed; set a trap for him in the fog. She had a gunman with her. He was supposed to kill Fenwick. But when Miss Valenska yelled, I knew something was haywire. She said Fenwick was really dead. I stopped the cameras. Then you showed up—"

I said: "Okay. That brings it up to now. Hop to the nearest phone. Call the cops. Get my friend Lieutenant Dave Donaldson of the homicide squad if you can. Tell him what happened. Tell him to flag his pants out here!"

Kinkaid stumbled away. I strode forward, lifted the Valenska frail in my arms.

She shrieked, clawed at my pan. "Let me alone! Let me go! Jeff isn't dead! He can't be dead! My kisses will bring him back—"

She was stark raving nuts. I slapped her across the puss; stung her as hard as I could. She blinked, gasped. Sanity returned to her dark eyes. "You—you—how dare you—!"

I said: "Take it easy, Miss Valenska. I'm Dan Turner, private snoop. I want to help you."

"Oh-h . . .! You're Dan Turner? Thank God, you're here! Jeff wanted you to protect him . . . Now I want you to find his murderer—"

Just then, out of the corner of my eye, I saw a movement. A tough-looking gazabo was edging off the set. He was sidling toward a fire-exit nearby. His hat was pulled low over his eyes. He had a three-day growth of whiskers on his mug. His coat collar was turned up. He had an automatic in his right fist.

He saw me looking at him. He broke into a run.

I turned Asta Valenska loose. She sagged back over Fenwick's body. I pivoted, plunged after the hard-looking lug.

He dropped his gat, added speed. A cameraman named Harry Treller got in his way. He slugged Treller a paste in the mouth, knocked him down. I tripped over the cameraman's gams, lost my balance.

Everybody else on the set seemed too paralyzed to do anything. By the time I got untangled and up on my pins again, the tough-faced gazabo had reached the fire-door. He leaped out into the night. The darkness ate him.

I pounded out after him. Something bashed down on my cranium. I saw a million red-and-blue Neon lights. Then I didn't see anything at all. I was out cold.

## CHAPTER III.
### Look for the Women

IT MUST have been all of ten minutes before I came to. Then I stood up.

I was groggy as hell. My knees were like jello. There was a lump on the back of my noggin the size of an army blimp. I had a headache built for an elephant.

But I didn't mind the pain. I was almost glad for it. A hell of a big load had been lifted off my mind.

I'd been biffed by the tough-faced mug. Why? There could be just one answer. He had killed Jeffery Fenwick, there on the set. It had to be that way. Otherwise, why had he lammed?

Okay. If he was the killer, that would leave the little blonde cutie from Trenton out of the mess entirely. It would put her in the clear. Deep inside me, I wanted her to be in the clear. I hated to think of her as a murderer. I wanted to believe that she'd kept her promise to me; that she'd given up her idea of bumping Fenwick.

By that time, there wasn't any use looking for the bird who had conked me. He'd had plenty of time to make his lam. I fumbled my way back inside the sound stage building; walked over on the set.

I saw a lot of uniformed coppers. Then I spotted my friend Dave Donaldson of the homicide detail. He had a medical examiner with him. They must have shown up while I was unconscious outside. The sawbones had already completed his examination of Jeffery Fenwick's corpse. Two bulls were carrying the body out on a stretcher.

Harry Treller, the cameraman, was rubbing his bruised jaw. He said: "Sorry I tripped you, Turner. That guy packed one hell of a wallop."

I said: "You're telling me?" and felt the swelling on the back of my skull. Then I asked: "Who was he,

Harry?"

"His name's Louie Frizzati. Bit-player. He was the thug that was supposed to shoot Fenwick—in the picture."

That told me plenty. I sprinted over to where Dave Donaldson was talking with Asta Valenska and Foster Kinkaid, the director.

Dave turned to me. "Where the hell have you been, Turner? I've questioned everybody but you. What—?"

I said: "I've been listening to the birdies. The murderer swatted me goofy."

"The murderer? You mean Frizzati, the bit-player?"

I said: "Yeah. The way I figure, he must have had some grudge against Fenwick. So he got himself cast as Fenwick's killer in the picture. Then he drilled him with a real slug."

The Valenska wren butted in. Her voice was harsh, vengeful. "No! You are wrong, Mr. Turner! Frizzati didn't do it! I know he didn't! It was some-body else. A woman!"

That almost floored me. Did Asta Valenska know anything about the blonde chicken? I said: "Wait a minute! If Frizzati was so damned innocent, why the hell did he take a powder?"

Donaldson grunted: "He was probably scared gut-less, that's all. I've got proof he didn't murder Fen-wick."

"Proof?" I barked.

"Sure." Donaldson hauled out the automatic that Frizzati had dropped when he lammed. "Look. The clip's loaded with blanks. Only one had been fired."

I said: "Maybe so. But there could have been a real pill in the firing-chamber."

Dave yanked back the breech-block. "Nix. If Frizzati had fired a genuine slug, the recall from the back-pressure would have worked the ejector, tossed out the empty shell. But the empty cartridge is still in the chamber—see? So it was a blank Frizzati fired. Blanks won't operate the 'ejector-mechanism. You know that."

I felt an all-gone sensation in my belly. Donaldson was right.

Asta Valenska said: "I tell you it was a woman who killed Jeff! A woman out of his past! She's been writing him threatening letters for the last two months. He was afraid of her. That's why he wanted Mr. Turner to work for him, protect him—"

Donaldson whirled on me. "So that's why you're mixed up in this, huh?"

I said: "Yeah." But I didn't tell him about my run-in with the yellow-haired Trenton lovely back in Fenwick's dressing-bungalow. Not just then. I still didn't think she was guilty. Maybe I was being a sentimental damned fool. But when I get a hunch, I play it through—until I find out I'm wrong, anyhow.

AN idea hit me. I looked at Foster Kinkaid. "How the hell could a strange dame get into this building?" I asked him. "Wouldn't she be stopped, questioned?"

Kinkaid nodded. "Usually. But she might have slipped inside, in the darkness."

I said: "Okay: For that matter how do we know Frizzati didn't have another roscoe on him. A roscoe loaded with real lead?"

Donaldson's pan turned red. "Damn it—I never thought of that! By God, I'll throw out a drag net for that guy. It might be an angle, Turner!" Then he stuck out his jaw. "But I still want to see those threatening letters that Fenwick got."

Asta Velenska said: "You and Mr. Turner can come home with me. I'll get them out of our wall-safe and show them to you."

Dave nodded. He issued some orders to his men. Then he and I and the Valenska wren went out to her waiting Rolls. We got in. The chauffeur headed for Beverly Hills.

The Fenwick-Valenska house was quite a stash. It was a big, two-story Spanish affair that must have cost a pile of geetus to build. Asta let us in; started upstairs. We trailed her. I couldn't help noticing the nifty way she moved under that clinging black dress. One moment it was as if she didn't have a muscle in her body; the next moment as if she were all muscle. I can't exactly describe it, but watching her did something to me. Her chiffon-sheathed stems were plenty shapely, too.

We reached the second floor. She opened the door of her boudoir; reached for the light-switch.

Out of the darkness a streak of flame stabbed at us. A roscoe said: *"Chow-chow!"* I felt a slug zip past my ear, bite into the woodwork. I dropped; pulled Asta Valenska down with me. My arm went around her. My hand brushed soft, velvety flesh through clinging silk.

She was so close to me that I couldn't get to the .32 automatic I always carry in a shoulder-holster. But I could hear Donaldson tugging out his rod.

Then there came another *"Chow-Chow!"* and two more orange flame spurts. Donaldson yeeped: "Damn it to hell! Nicked my gun hand!"

I heard a scuffling, scrambling sound across the room. Then three or four servants slamming up the stairs, yelling blue murder.

## CHAPTER IV.
### A Fee for Service

I HUGGED Asta Valenska close to me, kept her down out of gun-range. I could feel the warmth of her body against mine. Her heart was hammering like hell. She was shivering, moaning. Her panted breath was hot on my cheek.

Directly opposite, there was an open window. I could just barely see it in the darkness. Then

Donaldson got his service .38 shifted to his left hand. He cut loose with a blast that rattled the ceiling.

By the light from the flame-flashes that sprouted out from his gun-muzzle, I saw that the boudoir was empty. There was no answering fire, Dave found the light-button, flicked it. A pink lamp glowed into life.

I scrambled up, pulled Asta with me. Dave and I pelted to the window; saw a long ladder leading down to the ground. Then Miss Valenska screamed.

We whirled. She was pointing to a circular wall-safe beyond the bed. It was open, empty.

"Those threatening letters—gone! And Jeff had ten thousand dollars currency in there, too!" she gasped out.

Dave said: "Sure! The bimbo that killed him wanted to get her letters back. Wanted to clear her trail. We caught her in the act—so she burned some more gun-powder!" He glared at the servants. "Back downstairs, you people!" Then he straddled the window-sill. "You stay here, Turner! Keep your glims peeled! I'm going to find that dame or bust a gut!" He vanished down the ladder. I noticed that his right hand wasn't badly hurt; just creased across the knuckles.

The servants cleared out, chattering. Then something sagged against me. It was Asta Valenska. She had passed out!

I caught her, carried her over to the bed. Had one of those bullets plugged her? I loosened her belt, stripped her out of her dress. I rolled her over, put the focus on her.

She wasn't even scratched: She'd merely fainted.

She was a knockout, lying there. Her brief underthings covered one swell assortment of girl. All her curves and contours were delicious. Her hips had just the right flare. Her skin was as smooth and white as carved ivory. Her legs were prettier in real life than they were on the screen—and that's saying plenty!

I put my hand against her heart. It was beating slowly, steadily. My fingers tingled from the contact. And no damn wonder. Her skin was like warm satin —but a lot more thrilling. My blood began to simmer.

Her long, dark lashes fluttered. She parted her crimson lips. She looked up at me. "Oh-h-h—Mr. Turner—Dan—I'm f-frightened—!" Her arms went around my shoulders. She hauled me toward her. Maybe it was just her terror, but I got a kick out of it.

I whispered: "Take it easy, babe. You're Okay. Nothing's going to happen to you."

"But—but I'm scared! I w-won't feel easy until th-that terrible woman is caught and hanged ..."

I said: "Look. In the first place, how do we know it was a woman? It might have been Frizzati. Besides, what would the murderer have against you?"

"I—I d-don't know. She might hate me because I was married to J-Jeff ..." She clung to me, pressed herself as close as she could get. "Listen. I—I know everything about poor Jeff's past. He told me about being a taxi-driver, before he came to Hollywood. He t-told me how he got involved with some chippie back in Trenton—a waitress, she was. Maybe Jeff did wrong by leaving her in the lurch. I'm not trying to whitewash him. But she didn't have to kill herself!"

I didn't say anything. I just held her, let her go on talking.

SHE said: "Th-then the dead girl's sister found out that Jeff had become a movie star. That's when he began to get those th-threatening letters from Trenton. She said she was going to kill him. At first he didn't pay any attention to it. Then he began to worry. He confessed everything to me. I talked him into phoning you this evening. But it was ... too late! And now I'm afraid that g-girl will try to k-kill me, too!"

I patted her shoulder. "I think you're wrong. Anyhow, the cops will find the murderer."

"I—I haven't got any faith in the police. I want *you* to help!" she whimpered. "Whatever your fee is, I'll pay it!"

I hesitated. For some reason, I hated to consider starting out on the trail of the little blonde cutie. But after all, I'm in this game for the dough. I'm trying to save up enough lettuce to retire on, before some sharp apple engraves my name and address on a lead slug. And besides, if I took up the chase independently, I might find the trail leading to somebody else besides the Trenton chicken. Louie Frizzati, for example.

I must have studied it over for maybe two or three whole minutes. Asta Valenska misunderstood my silence. She probably figured I was going to turn her down. Because she suddenly squeezed herself tight against me and whispered: "You must help me! You *must!*" She grabbed my hand, squeezed it, carried it to her cheek.

I felt the silky texture of her skin. I looked down at her; soaked up the gorgeous radiance of her alluring form. She raised her head, snaked an arm around my neck, pressed her crimson lips against my mouth.

I could feel the warmth of her breath, the soft quiver of her lips. I hadn't expected that sort of fee. But when it was tossed in my lap that way ... Well, what the hell? There are times when a man can't helping skidding.

I skidded.

I crushed her in my arms; planted a red-hot kiss on her throat. It lasted a damned long time. My hand slipped down her back, held her so closely that I almost cracked her ribs. Under my palm I felt the muscles of her back ripple as she clung to me, trembling. I wasn't any too steady, myself. There's six-feet-three of me, and every inch was full of tingling sensation. I got a little dizzy then, forgot all about murders . . . everything ... .

I RECOVER quick. It wasn't much later when I said: "Well, baby, you've hired a private detective. I'll see that you don't regret it."

She scribbled in her check-book, handed me a ticket for a grand. I left her, went downstairs. I climbed into her Rolls, told the chauffeur to haul me back to the Altamount lot where I'd left my own jalopy.

On the way, I mulled things over. I still couldn't see why that Louis Frizzati lug had acted the way he did—unless he was up to his ears in the case somehow. I decided to check up on him, for a starter.

At the Altamount lot I dismissed the Valenska chariot. I went inside, hunted around for Foster Kinkaid. He was still there. I said: "Listen, Fos. You directed this last picture of Fenwick's. What do you know about Frizzati?"

"Not much. Jeffery Fenwick himself asked me to give Frizzati a bit in the opus."

I said: "The hell you preach! Did you tell that to Lieutenant Donaldson?"

Kinkaid's pleasant map was creased with a frown. "Why, no. He didn't ask me. I didn't think of it 'til just now."

"Okay. Maybe you can give me Frizzati's address,

huh?"

"I think so." Kinkaid took me into his office. He thumbed through some records. "Here it is." He named a cheap walk-up apartment on Los Feliz.

I thanked him, went out again. I climbed into my own coupe. Before heading for Los Feliz, I decided to go home to change my clothes. The suit I was wearing was all torn, muddy, where I'd taken a couple of headers back on that sound stage. Besides, I wanted a snort of Vat 69 to brace me up.

I parked in front of my stash, went up to my apartment. I unlocked the door, started to open it. Then I froze.

Somebody was in there!

## CHAPTER V.
### Red Hair—Henna!

I MADE a dive for my roscoe, yanked it out. Then I kicked my door open; flattened myself against the jamb. I snarled: "Stick 'em up!"

Somebody wailed: "No—don't shoot—!" and a light came on.

I felt my eyes getting wide. A wave of surprise reached up and slugged me in the whiskers. I stared at a crouched, white-faced, yellow-haired lovely shivering against the far wall.

It was the Trenton cutie!

I said: "For God's sake!" I slammed the door behind me, walked toward her. "What the purple hell are you doing here?" Then I grabbed her, started frisking her for the pearl-handled gat.

Her coat was off. Her dress was still torn, the way I'd last seen her in Jeffery Fenwick's dressing-bungalow. Frankly, it was a pleasure, frisking her for that roscoe. But she didn't have it. I searched twice, to make sure, and I made a good job of it. That's me—thorough!

She stood still for it, submissive but not to well pleased. Didn't wiggle—didn't shrink. She just said: "Go ahead. Search me. I haven't got a g-gun."

"Jeff isn't dead!" she screamed. "My kisses will bring him back—!" She was raving mad. I slapped her across the puss.

I backed away, found her discarded coat. No roscoe there, either. I said: "What did you do with it af-

ter you killed Fenwick?"

She got even whiter. "I didn't kill him!" she panted. Her eyes looked wild. "I didn't! *I didn't!* Th-that's why I came here ... I heard the newsboys yelling their extras about Fenwick being m-murdered ..."

I said: "Quiet down. Start at the beginning. And tell me the truth, or I'll slap the living hell out of you!" I meant it, too.

She shuddered. For a minute I thought she was going to fold over. I went to my cellarette, hauled out a fifth of Vat 69. I poured two stiff jorums; gave her one. I downed the other myself. I needed it.

She choked the fire-water past her gullet. Then she said: "You've got to believe me, Mr. Turner! You've just got to! You're the only one I can turn to. You told me your name, back in that bungalow. And when I learned that Fenwick was d-dead, I came here to you for help. I c-climbed in through your fire-escape window ..."

I said: "What a minute. First of all, where did you go when you left Fenwick's dressing-quarters?"

"I—I took a bus and w-went downtown."

"And why did you swipe your revolver back out of my pocket before you left?" I snapped at her.

Crimson stained her cheeks. "You convinced me that I should forget my hate for Jeffery Fenwick. I decided to go back east, as you advised. But I—I was broke. I'd spent my last money for train-fare to California. I didn't have a return ticket. Then I thought maybe I could sell my clothing, my luggage ..."

"What's that got to do with the revolver?"

She said: "Before I could get my bags out of the hotel room, I'd have to pay my room-rent. I didn't have the money. So I thought I'd pawn the g-gun for a few dollars. That would release my luggage, so I could sell—"

I broke in "You heisted the gat so you could hock it?"

"Y'yes."

"Well, did you?"

She nodded. "I pawned it the minute I got downtown."

I said: "Where's the ticket?"

She pointed toward her purse on a chair. I grabbed it, opened it. I found a pawn-ticket. "That's it," she told me.

I said: "Okay. You say you soaked the gun as soon as you got downtown, huh?"

"Yes."

"Hm-m-. If you're telling me the truth, it spells plenty. It means you weren't the one who petered Asta Valenska's wall-safe and took those potshots at me."

She stared at me. "Wall-safe? I—don't understand!"

"You wouldn't—if you're really leveling with me. Now look. Somebody croaked Jeffery Fenwick. If it wasn't you, then it must have been Louie Frizzati."

The minute I said that, she slumped into a chair. Her mouth opened wide. "Did—did you say *Frizzati?*"

I had a hunch I was about to learn something important. I said: "Yeah. Louie Frizzati. Know him?"

SHE tottered toward me, grabbed my arm. "Louie Frizzati was a friend of Jeffery Fenwick! Back in Trenton! Frizzati was a taxi-driver, too. And a—a criminal. He and Fenwick were pals. They stole money from drunks who rode in their cabs. My sister knew about it. She told me. She tried to get Fenwick to break away from Frizzati..."

My blood began to race. "So Fenwick and Frizzati were buddies!" I whispered. "Now I can see why Fenwick got Frizzati a job in pictures! Frizzati knew too much about him—his past. He was probably blackmailing Fenwick!"

She said: "Maybe that's it! And maybe Fenwick refused to pay any more money—so Louie k-killed him!"

It sounded like sense. It added up. But it all depended on whether or not the blonde cutie was telling the truth.

I said: "Sweetness, I'm going to check on you—and God help you if you've lied!" Then I grabbed her, carried her into my bedroom.

"Wh-what are you d-doing to me ...?" she wailed.

"Fixing things so you won't lam while I'm gone!" I

said. "You're going to get undressed and I'm going to lock up your clothes."

"I—I—"

"Look. If you haven't got anything to wear, you won't take a powder on me," I said. "Are *you* going to take 'em off, or should I?"

"I—I'll do whatever you say. T-turn your back," she whispered.

I faced away from her. A couple of frilly bits of silk landed at my feet. Then I heard my bed creak.

When I turned, she was under the covers. Only her bare arms and shoulders were showing. My fingers itched; but I didn't go near her. I just gathered up her duds, blew her a kiss, walked out of the bedroom. I locked her in and put her clothes in a closet.

I tossed another snort of Scotch down the hatch for good luck. I made sure I had that pawn-ticket for her roscoe. Then I went out.

The hockshop was an all-night joint on Main Street. I drove down there, ankled in. I said: "Uncle, I want to ask you about a gat." I flashed my tin, shoved the ticket under his nose.

He looked at it. "Vell, vat about it? It is vor a bearl-handled rofolfer. A young voman bawned it tonight. I gafe her vour dollars."

"What time was it?"

"Aboud eight-thirdy, guarder to nine."

I could have kissed him. Now I knew the yellow-haired wren was leveling with me. If she'd put her rod in soak at that hour, she couldn't have got back out to Beverly Hills in time to rob Asta Valenska's safe, crease Donaldson with a slug. And even if she'd had time, she couldn't have done the shooting—because she didn't have her gun.

I went out, climbed back into my wreck. I headed out toward Glendale; swung into Los Feliz. That's where Louie Frizzati lived, according to Foster Kinkaid.

TWENTY minutes later I drew up before the address Kinkaid has given me. The joint was a cheap, shabby two-story building of weatherbeaten frame. I jammed my thumb against the bell-button.

Pretty soon a big, hulking slob opened the door, stared out at me. He was almost as tall as I am. He must have weighed a good three hundred pounds. He was hog-fat. He had a patch over one eye. He looked like a pirate.

I said: "Good evening, cousin. Are you the manager of this stash?"

"Yeah. So what? And I ain't your cousin."

I said: "Okay. But how about slipping me a few minutes of your valuable time? I'm looking for a lug named Fizzati." As I spoke, I shoved my way into the hall.

The one-eyed hombre tried to block me. "Lay off, shamus. I don't know nothin' about Frizzati. He ain't here. I've talked to enough cops tonight. They been buzzin' like bees. Reporters, too. If Frizzati's in a jam, the hell with him. I don't know nothin' about him."

I said: "So the bulls have been here, have they? Maybe a lard-puss gumshoe named Donaldson, too; huh?"

"Yeah. He was here. Now g'wan. Take it on the lam."

"Donaldson didn't find any trace of Frizzati?"

One-Eye said: "I already told you Frizzati aint been home tonight. Cert'nly Donaldson didn't find him. Are you goin' to blow, or shall I belt you a few?"

I said: "Wait a minute, friend. You've got me all wrong. I'm no bull. I'm Frizzati's friend. He's in a tight spot. It's a bump-off beef, no fooling."

"So which?"

"So I've got some dough for him. Enough to take him to China if he wants to go there. Be a good guy and tell me where you think he might be. Give me a lead. You don't want Louie to get his neck stretched, do you?"

The big guy snarled: "You're a damn' liar, that's what you are. You're no friend of Frizzati's. I never seen you here before." Then he took a poke at my kisser.

He almost caught me with my pants at half-mast. I just barely ducked his fist. Then I waded into him.

I slammed a load of knuckles into his teeth. Then I buried my left duke wrist-deep in his porky belly.

He said: "O-oo-oooff-fff—!" and belched in my face. He smelled like stale beer. I spat, lowered my head, got in close. I whammed hell out of him.

He ate three more pokes as if they'd been ice cream. Then he managed to cork me on the pan— just over the cheekbone. His fist felt like a pile-driver. It drove my noggin so far back I could see the floor upside-down.

I staggered. My shoulder-blades smacked into the wall. Before I could get set again, the big duck had me.

He said: "I'll tear your liver out an' fry it for breakfast!" His arms pinned mine to my ribs. Then he reached up, started to jab his thumb into my left eyeball.

I don't like guys to do that to me. I raised my knee, drove it into his guts.

He curled over, grabbed himself. I blinked the tears out of my glims. Then I went to work on him. I didn't want to cork him unconscious. I just wanted to make him ache all over. I started lacing him with both fists. I twisted my knuckles around, every time they landed on his greasy lug. I split the skin on his cheeks, cut him into pieces. He bled like a pig.

Pretty soon he went down, blubbering. "Don't hit me no more! I can't take it!" His voice was a high whine.

I said: "All right. What about Frizzati? Do you know where I might find him?"

"No!"

I drew my foot back. "How would you like some shoeleather, my friend?" I booted him in the ribs.

Once was enough. He squealed: "Lay off! I—I'll talk!"

I said: "Sure you'll talk. I knew it all the time. Commence, pal."

"Louie runs around with a bim named Dolly Devorely. Extra wren at Cosmotone. I dunno where she lives. But she's his sweetie. He hangs around her stash most of the time. Maybe he's there now; I wouldn't know. That's all I can tell you."

I said: "Much obliged, Blubber. I'll look her up. If you've steered me wrong, God have mercy on you." I dragged him into a back room where there was a dirty bed. I ripped a sheet into strips, tied him up plenty tight. That was to keep him from getting in touch with Frizzati with a warning.

Then I pulled out my rod, tapped him over the noggin with the soft end. Not hard enough to crush his skull. Just enough to put him to dreamland for an hour or so.

I went out.

AT the nearest drug-store, I parked again. I went in to a phone-booth, thumbed through the directory. I couldn't find any Dolly Devorely listed. She wasn't in the city directory, either.

But I still had an angle. I dropped a buffalo, dialed a friend of mine who runs a casting agency. When he answered, I said: "Hi, Tom. This is Dan Turner. I'm calling you because Central Casting is closed at night. Have you got a frill on your list by the name of Dolly Devorely?"

He said: "Wait a minute till I look it up." Then he came back to the phone. "Yeah. I got a Dorothy Devorely. Age twenty-six. Red hair—henna. Five foot even. Plenty of curves in the right places. Nice stems. Works at Cosmotone, mostly. Want her phone-number?"

"Just her address," I said.

He gave it to me. It was a bungalow court off Sunset.

I said: "Thanks a million, Tom." Then I went out, slammed myself into my coupe. I headed hell-for-leather toward Sunset.

## CHAPTER VI.
### Death Strikes Again

I MADE shredded wheat out of my tires, braking to a stop a block south of Dolly Devorely's bungalow court. I made sure my gat was loose in its holster. Then I walked the remaining distance to the red-haired extra girl's front door.

Her cottage was at the rear of the court. The shades were down, but I saw a splinter of light around them. Somebody was home.

I knocked.

It was a couple of minutes before the door opened. Then a flame-tressed, nicely built little bimbo opened up for me. She was wearing thin green pajamas. The light was behind her, and I didn't have to use my imagination to figure out her shape. She wasn't hard on the eyes *at* all.

I shoved my roscoe against her middle. I said: "How would you like a dimple in your tummy?"

She gasped, backed away. I followed her, closed the door with my heel. She whimpered: "Wh-what do you want? Put that gun away, for God's sake!"

"After a while, kiddo. Not yet. Where's Louie?"

"L-Louie who?"

"Don't feed me that. Louie Frizzati. That's who."

"I—I don't know any Louie Frizzati."

I said: "Swell. That gives me an excuse to get rough with you." I edged in her direction.

She backed away. "Lay off me! I don't—I haven't—"

"Sure you won't. Of course you haven't. You're dumb. You'll be dumber when I get finished with you. You'll be needing some new teeth." I made a grab for her with my free hand.

She tried to jerk away. Her pajama-jacket tore. It hadn't concealed much in the first place, and now the rents in it disclosed even more. My eyes bulged.

She tried to cover herself with her hands, but no woman ever had hands large enough to take in that much territory. "If you put your paws on me, I—I'll scream!" she panted.

I said: "Go ahead. Then you'll wake up screaming for the devil to let you into hell. I'd just as soon shoot you as look at you."

"You—you wouldn't dare."

"You don't know me. Come on, darling, before I lose my temper. What about Louie Frizzati?"

She said: "He—he isn't here!" Her eyes darted toward a closed door on the other side of the room.

"Oh. So you admit you know him, after all?"

"Y-yes. But I—I haven't seen him for several days. Honest I haven't."

I said: "Sweetheart, you're a liar. But I know a way to make you come clean. We're going to have some fun!" I put away my roscoe, circled my arms around her. I made sure she was between me and the closed door. I had a hunch Louie Frizzati was in that next room. But he wouldn't dare shoot at me as long as Dolly Devorely was in the way. However, he most likely would show himself if I carried out the plan I had in mind.

I kissed the red-haired bim right on the mouth.

At the same time, I caught both her wrists, imprisoned them behind her with my left hand. Then I went to work on her. I mauled her with my hands. I put plenty on the ball; let her understand that I wasn't kidding.

She yipped: "No—no! Louie—for God's sake help

me—"

THE closed door opened. That's what I was expecting. I whipped out my automatic, aimed it. I said: "Okay, Frizzati. Come out with your hands up high. I mean business. I owe you something for the way you swatted me on the Altamount lot tonight, anyhow."

Frizzati walked into the room. He looked green around the dewlaps. He said: "Listen, copper—for Gawd's sake—"

"Stow it. You croaked Jeffery Fenwick. You damned near plugged me and Donaldson and Asta Valenska, later, in Valenska's boudoir. Better save your alibi for a mouthpiece!"

His eyes looked glassy. "You're wrong, copper!" he jabbered. "I never bumped Fenwick! I lammed because I figgered I might be framed for it. But I didn't cool him! Listen—I admit I petered that safe in Valenska's bedroom. I knew Fenwick had dough there. I needed it to make a get-away. But I never put the trigger to him. He was croaked by—"

That was the last thing Louie Frizzati ever said. From the window behind him, a gun poked under the drawn blind. It went: *"Blooey—Blooey—Blooey!"*

Frizzati dropped. So did Dolly Devorely. The third slug grazed my left shoulder, burned me as it ripped through my coat sleeve.

I smacked the floor with my belly; put four fast

ones through that flapping blind. It rolled up with a hell of a clatter. But there was nobody outside. I had heated up my cannon for nothing; wasted four perfectly good chunks of lead.

I snaked my way to the window; took a chance on peering out. All I saw was a vacant lot and a night full of shadows.

## CHAPTER VII.
## The Cutie from Trenton

I DIVED FOR the ground outside, landed on my hands and knees. I picked myself out of a flower-bed, started running. But I didn't know which the hell way to run. Then, in the distance, I heard the whine of a motor; the smooth purr of meshed gears. Tortured tires screeched around a corner, faded away.

That was that.

I scrambled back into Dolly's living-room. Dolly herself was on her back. Blood was seeping from a hole in her breast. I felt her wrist. No pulse. She was as dead as a pork-chop.

Louie Frizzati lay beyond her. I looked him over. The top of his skull was ripped open. His brains were all over the floor.

There was a phone in the corner. I grabbed it, dialed police headquarters. "Lieutenant Donaldson—quick!" I said.

Pretty soon Dave's voice answered. "Yeah?"

"Dan Turner calling. Two more bump-offs for you. Louie Frizzati and his moll." I gave him the address.

He said: "I'll be double-damned to hell! How in God's name did you—?"

"Cork it up till you get here," I said. I hung up.

The whole damn court was alive by this time. People were pounding on the bungalow's front door. I opened it, flashed my badge. "There's been a shooting folks. Beat it. Go on back home." I slammed the door in their faces.

While I was waiting for Donaldson, I went back to the window; flashed my pencil light on the ground below. Maybe there were footprints in the soft loam of the flower-bed, I thought. Perhaps the killer had left some trace.

But no soap. If there had been any prints, I'd wiped them out by landing on all fours when I dived over the sill. Beyond the flower-bed, the ground was hard as concrete.

I fumbled for a gasper, set fire to it. I took a deep drag. I was wishing to God I'd brought a flask of Vat 69 along with me. My nerves were all raw. I went into the kitchen, found a half-pint of rye in the cabinet. I don't like rye, but it's better than nothing. I killed it in three swallows. Then I felt a little better.

My left arm stung. I took off my coat, looked myself over. I wasn't bleeding. But there was a big red welt across my muscle. The bullet had come to damn close for comfort!

PRETTY soon I heard sirens wailing, brakes screaming. Dave Donaldson came roaring into the room. "Turner—what in the blue blazes—"

I said: "Have a look yourself. Frizzati has joined his ancestors. So has his lady-love." I pointed to the two corpses on the floor.

"But how the hell did you find Frizzati?" Donaldson rasped. "Damn it. I've had a dragnet out for him all night!"

I said: "You didn't use the right methods. I beat hell out of a guy to get my information. But it didn't do me much good."

"What do you mean by that?"

I said: "Frizzati was just going to tell me who croaked Jeffery Fenwick. But a bullet shut him up before he got the words out of his kisser."

Dave blinked as if I'd slugged him. "Frizzati was going to tell—Say, Turner, are you uts-nay?"

"Not any more than usual. Listen. Before he kicked the bucket, Louie confessed something to me. He admitted that he was the one who robbed the safe in Asta Valenska's boudoir." I went to my knees alongside Louie's body; felt in his pockets. I dragged out a packet of century notes and some letters. "This proves it," I grunted.

Donaldson said: "For God's sake!! I'll say it proves

it! It also proves he bumped Fenwick on that sound stage!"

"Nix. You're all haywire there, Dave. Get this straight. Louie Frizzati and Jeffery Fenwick had been pals, back east. Crooks, too, in a small way. Rolling drunks, and that sort of thing. Well, Fenwick comes to California; landed in the movies. He became a star. Frizzati showed up. So Fenwick got him a job in pictures. Bit parts. That was probably to keep Frizzati from spilling anything about Fenwick's past life. Fenwick didn't want that kind of publicity. It would have spoiled his career as a great screen lover."

Dave said: "All right. Keep on talking."

"Well," I went on, "tonight Fenwick got taken with lead poisoning on that Altamount set. Louie had a good idea who the killer was. But he was afraid he might get framed for the job, himself. With his criminal record, it looked like a lousy situation to him. So he lammed."

"Yeah. Then what?"

I said: "Louie needed dough for a get-away. He knew Fenwick had a sweet pile of lettuce in a wall-safe at home. So he burgled his way into his dead pal's house, petered the safe. In the darkness, he grabbed everything his hands touched. Including these threatening letters. Then he started to take a powder when you and Miss Valenska and I showed up. He took a couple of shots at us to scare us back, give him time to lam."

Dave looked at his bandaged knuckles; then at Louie's corpse. He growled: "Damn it. I was hoping I'd have a chance to bat him a few for nicking me." Then, suddenly, he whirled at me. "Say, Dan, damn it—"

"Yes?"

"You realize what this means? It means the bird who croaked Fenwick is still loose! That dame from back east—the one who wrote those notes to him — she's the one! By God, she must be a homicidal maniac! First she cools Fenwick. Then she learns that Louie Frizzati is wise to her. So she comes here and burns him down along with his moll!"

I SHOOK my head. "Nope. All wrong, Dave. She couldn't have done it."

"How do you know?" he blatted.

"In the first place she was hocking her gun around the time Fenwick was rubbed out on the set. In the second place, she couldn't have come here and killed Louie and his sweetie—because I've got her locked in my apartment!"

I thought he was going to poke me in the puss. "You—you've got her in your flat? Why, you lousy, double-crossing—"

I said: "Hold it, Dave. Calm down. I tell you I left her in my apartment—without any duds. She isn't twins. She couldn't be in two places at once. She can't be the one that rubbed out Frizzati and Dolly Devorely just now. And besides, she hocked her gun around eight-thirty this evening. So she couldn't have bumped Fenwick, either."

"Yeah? Maybe she had a second roscoe that you didn't know about!" Donaldson snarled. "Come on— we're going to your dive. I'm putting the nippers on that bimbo!"

I said: "Okay, if that's the way you feel about it. She'll probably be safer in the clink until morning, anyway. There's a killer loose, and you never know who's going to get it next."

Just then, before we'd even looked at the letters Frizzati stole from Valenska, some of Donaldson's homicide flatties showed up. The medical examiner was with them. Dave growled some orders. Then he and I ankled down the street to my parked jalopy.

I drove home.

We went upstairs to my door. Dave said: "I'm going to throw this dame into a cell so fast her toenails will curl!"

I turned the key in the lock. We walked in. Everything looked exactly the way I'd left it—until I took a gander at the bedroom door.

It was wide open.

I said: "What the hell—!" and dived over the threshold into the bedroom. I felt suddenly sick.

The yellow-haired cutie from Trenton was gone.

## CHAPTER VIII.
### The Secret of Infra-Red

THE bed was mussed and the covers were turned back. The window to the fire-escape was open. I made a quick frisk of the flat. My bathrobe was missing from the closet. There was no trace of the blonde kid.

Dave Donaldson said: "I ought to put the pinch on you for obstructing justice and aiding a criminal, you damn interfering numbskull!"

"But look, Dave—!" I yipped. "I figured she was innocent. I had no idea—"

"Sure not. You never have any ideas!" he grated. "You're just a plain sap. I can see what happened. The frill made a chump out of you. She sucked you in. She's the murderer—and you let her get away. If you'd called me the minute you got your mitts on her, Louie Frizzati and the Devorely moll would be alive right now!"

I said: "Maybe you're right. I'm sorry."

"Sorry, my eyebrow! Now I've got to throw out the dragnet for a dame I never saw. I don't even know what she looks like. A swell job you dished up for me, damn you."

I lighted a pill. "Go ahead and rave. I don't blame you. But at least I can give you her description." Then I gave him a quick word picture of the yellow-haired lovely.

He drank it all in with his ears. Then he said: "Okay. I'm starting out. And for God's sake, stay the hell off this case from now on. You louse it up every time you stick your beak into it." He stormed out.

I went into my living room, tossed two slugs of Vat 69 down my throat. Then I went back and sat on my bed. I felt lousy. I'm too damned old to entertain many illusions about the so-called human race. But that blonde cutie had pulled the wool over my glims—plenty. For once, I'd made a hell of a mistake about somebody's character.

Maybe five minutes passed. Then all of a sudden I heard a chocked voice whispering: "So you t-turned against me...!"

I shot off that bed as if the mattress had been full of rattlesnakes. I whirled—and saw the yellow-haired baby standing at the door of the bathroom!

She was wearing my dressing gown. It trailed around her feet, fell open at the throat where her body began to lift in lilting dizzying curves. Her eyes were blue pools of accusation.

I said: "For the love of God—!"

"I was hiding in your soiled clothes hamper in the bathroom," she said.

"You—you were there all the time?"

She said: "Yes. After you left, I got up and wandered around. Your bathroom door-key worked the lock of the bedroom door. I wanted a cigarette. So I let myself into the living room to look for one. I was sitting there when I heard you coming back. I—I heard that other man say he was going to p-put me

"Get busy," I said. "If you don't have any clothes, I know you'll be here when I come back." Pretty soon, a frilly bit of silk landed beside me. . . .

in a cell. So I ran into the bathroom and hid myself."

I grabbed her. I said: "Sweetness, I'm going to kiss hell out of you!" And I did.

She broke loose. "L-let me alone! I—I hate you! You think I'm a murderer!"

I said: "No I don't. Not now. I know you're innocent. And I'm starting out to prove it. I'm going to clear you of this mess, by God!"

"B-but I *am* clear!" she wailed. "If you checked with that pawnbroker you know I didn't—"

"Yeah," I nodded. "But I'm not the law. Dave Donaldson is the guy I've got to convince. He probably wouldn't believe me if I told him you were right here in my bathroom all the time. He'd say I was just fronting for you, lying to save your neck. Three people have been burned down tonight. And the only way I can get you out is to find the real killer."

She came close to me; put her arms around me. "Th-then you w-will . . save me?"she shivered.

I held her, kissed her again. My bath-robe was *much* too big for her. Her skin was like whipped cream. She was warm and soft and delicious as she melted against me. Her lips were moist, trembling with eagerness.

I let her go. I said: "Baby, I want you to promise me you'll stay right here until I come back. Will you?"

"I—I'll be waiting for you," she answered softly.

MURDER ON THE SOUND STAGE

There was a hint of promise in her voice. It did something to my veins. I scrammed out before I lost control ...

DOWNSTAIRS I piled into my heap. I had two reasons for finding Jeffery Fenwick's killer, now, I had to earn the grand that Asta Valenska had given me. And I had to clear the blonde kiddo.

Everything went back to that sound stage set on the Altamount lot. That's where Fenwick had been burned down. Then, later, the heat had been put to Louie Frizzati—because Louie knew too much and was going to spill his guts.

I kept thinking about the sound stage. Somebody on that set had bumped Fenwick. Who?

An idea kicked me in the pants. I said: "Maybe—!" Then I gunned the glands out of my motor. I headed for the home of my friend Harry Treller, the Altamount cameraman.

He lived in a house off Crenshaw. He was a bachelor. It wasn't quite eleven-thirty when I rang his bell. But he was in bed. He was in pajamas when he let me in.

I said: "Hi, Harry. How's the jaw?"

He rubbed his bruise. "Aches like hell. I'd like to get a poke at the Frizzati lug."

"No chance. He's dead," I said.

"What—?'

"Yeah. He got rubbed out by the same person that

killed Jeffery Fenwick. He knew too much. Now look. You can help me if you will. I want to see the rushes of that last scene Fenwick acted in. The scene where he was cooled off. Can you get the rush print and run it off in a projector for me?"

Harry said: "We'd have to get an order from Foster Kinkaid."

"Okay. Get dressed and we'll hunt him up."

I followed Treller into his bedroom. He started climbing into his togs. I noticed a framed cabinet photograph on his bureau. It was a picture of Asta Valenska. It was inscribed: "All my heart's love to Harry. Your Asta V." The date on it was two years old.

I said: "I didn't know you and Asta were sweet on each other."

"It didn't last," he grunted. "She married Fenwick instead. But we're still good friends. I'd go to hell for her, any day. Come on, let's go."

We crawled into my coupe. I drove out to Wilshire to the Gayboy Arms, where Foster Kinkaid had a suite. Kinkaid's gu-gu valet let us in. Then Kinkaid himself strolled out of his bedroom. He said: "Hello, Turner. Treller. What's up now?"

I told him I wanted to see the the rushes of Jeffery Fenwick's last movie scene.

He said: "Sure. But I'm afraid it won't show much. It was fog stuff, you know. I deliberately shot the action so that nothing but blurred shapes would appear. But we'll take a look, anyhow."

He got dressed. Then all three of us drove down to the Altamount lot.

Kinkaid went into the lab building. That department worked all night at Altamount, developing negs and making rush prints for viewing the next morning. In ten minutes or so, Kinkaid came back with four flat, round cans. He said: "These will be silent, of course. The sound-track is synchronized on later. Of course I can find the play-back record and run it off too, if you like. But it mightn't match up exactly with the action."

I said: "Never mind the sound. It's the action I want to see."

We went into a small projection room in the executive building. Harry Treller ran the projector. He threaded a reel into the machine. Kinkaid stood alongside me. I stared at the screen.

It glowed with white, glaring light. Then the picture started.

There was an eerie, ghostly quality about it. The abandoned house loomed faintly through the drifting artificial fog. Jeffery Fenwick walked on-stage. He was close enough to be recognized through the mists. It was like looking at a dead man's ghost.

Then he turned away from the lens; edged back toward the rear of the set. I could see only his outlines now, like a wraith. There was a suspicion of movement over to the left, where the fog was thickest.

"That's where Miss Valenska and Louie Frizzati were crouching down," Kinkaid whispered to me. Then he said: "If you look close enough, you'll see two other faces at a downstairs window of the house. There were two extra girls who were supposed to be prisoners. They're staring toward Fenwick."

I kept my glims glued on the screen. Sure enough, I tabbed two frills through a fog-eddy. Then the mist obscured them.

Kinkaid said: "Now the shooting. But all you'll see is a streak of flame. The Hays office won't allow us to show an actual murder, right out plain. That's why I used fog to obscure the action."

AS he spoke, a dull lick of fire glimmered through the fag. I saw it vague shadow-shape crumple and fall. That was Jeffery Fenwick—dead.

Then the reel ended in a square of white brilliance that almost blinded me.

Kinkaid said: "I stopped the cameras when Asta screamed. That's all of it."

I turned to Harry Treller at the projector. "Four cameras were working, weren't they?"

"Yes."

"Run off one of the other reels, then."

He said: "Okay," and threaded a new film into the dingus. This time I saw the scene from another angle. The shot had been made from one of the camera-cranes. It was an overhead shot, looking down at the set from a high angle.

But the action was just the same as before. At the time of Fenwick's death, the fake fog was like pea-soup. All I could see was shadow-shapes. I couldn't identify any one of them individually.

The reel stopped. Foster Kinkaid said: "What were you hoping to find, Turner?"

I said: "Another streak of flame."

"What do you mean?"

"Well, we know Frizzati fired a blank. That shows on the film. But he didn't shoot a real slug. The bullet that killed Fenwick came from another gun. I was hoping to find out where the second gun was fired from. But it didn't work."

Treller said: "Shall I run off these other two reels? They'll both show the same thing you just looked at."

"Never mind," I told him. "Thanks just the same." I took the four flat cans from him.

Kinkaid said: "Is it your opinion that Fenwick was plugged by someone on the set?"

"Either on the set—or just outside the camera lines, hiding," I answered.

"Too bad we weren't using infra-red negative," he mused. "That penetrates murk. It might have shown the extra flame-streak you're looking for. Well—anything else, Turner?"

"No. We may as well go home," I told him.

I drove him to the Gayboy Arms. Then I took Harry Treller back to his house near Crenshaw. After that, I started cruising nowhere in particular. I was up a stump. A theory was forming in the back of my noggin. But theories aren't any good unless they're backed by conclusive proof, definite evidence. And that's what I didn't have.

## CHAPTER IX.
### Synthetic Movies

ALL OF A sudden an idea hit me. I remembered something Foster Kinkaid had said.

"By God!" I whispered.

I jerked my wheel around, fed my engine all the soup she'd gobble. I headed for Westwood.

After a while I drew up before a big, splendiculous mansion. It was the home of Sol Levering, general manager of Altamount Pix. I raced up on his porch, rang.

A blinky-eyed butler answered. "Yes, sir?"

"I want to see Mr. Levering. Police business." I gave him a gander at my badge.

He let me in; went upstairs. Pretty soon Sol Levering came down, rubbing his glims and yawning. He said: "Why—Turner! What the devil—?"

"Listen, Sol. This is important. Asta Valenska hired me to find Jeff Fenwick's killer. I think I've got a hot lead. But I'm going to need one hell of a lot of assistance."

"I'll help if I can, Dan," Sol said slowly.

"Swell. Now look. This whole thing's got to be done fast—and kept absolutely mum. In the first place, can you name me three wrens that can be trusted? Frills with screen experience, preferably. And if possible, girls who went for Fenwick in a great big way."

Levering frowned. Then he said: "That should be easy. Fenwick had a whole harem of nifties all over Hollywood. You know what his reputation was. He was quite a chaser."

"So I've heard. Well?"

Sol said: "There's Vio Yorkalle, for one. She's a honey."

I nodded. I knew Vio Yorkalle. I'd been on parties with her. She was a cute, chestnut-haired filly with a ton of sex-appeal. I said: "Okay. I'll get Vio. Who else?"

"Well, how about Mayda Carman? And Lola Lemoine?"

"I've met 'em both. They'll do." I jotted down the three names and addresses. Then I said: "The rest is going to be up to you. I'll need a cameraman—but not Harry Treller. He isn't to hear a word about this thing. I should have a director, too. Maybe you could handle that job. You used to carry a mega-phone in your early days, didn't you?"

He said: "Sure. But what—"

"Dave? Dan Turner calling. Two more bump-offs for you. Yeah . . . Frizzati and his moll."

"I'll also want two men. Actors. And one property-man to work the fog-machine."

Levering blinked. "What the devil are you up to? You sound as if you wanted to make a movie."

I said: "That's it exactly. I'm going to shoot a duplicate of that scene where Jeffery Fenwick was murdered. Only I'll be using a substitute cast. How about it?"

"Well, all right. If you think it'll do any good, I'll work with you. But who are you after? What's the idea? Can't you let me in on it?"

I said: "Not just now. Meet me in an hour, on Sound Stage 'A'—that'll give you time enough to round up the men you'll need. I'll bring the girls."

He nodded. I left him, went back to my jalopy. I drove to the apartment where Vio Yorkalle hung out.

VIO let me in when I knocked. She'd been asleep. She wore the thinnest night-gown a silkworm ever turned out. Like cellophane! And what a shape that baby had! What legs; what hips; what . . . I began to forget all about business . . .

She opened her eyes wide. "Well, throw me down a chute if it isn't Sherlock Turner—in the flesh!"

I grinned, blinking, went in. Speaking of flesh— but why speak of it?" I said. I grabbed her, pulled her toward me, fed her a kiss.

She panted: "Golly! What's the rush, Handsome? You might at least give me time to get set." Then she said: "Where've you been all my life and what's on your mind?"

"You are, just now," I told her.

"Quit kidding. I know you. You want something."

I said: "Sure I do. This." I kissed her again; her lips parted a little under mine.

One of her shoulder-straps started to skid. An inch or so of white skin popped invitingly into view. I dropped my lips to her shoulder.

She started to quiver. She was getting interested, no fooling! She said: "Mm-m-m-m ...! Nice!"

I grinned into her hazel eyes. "Like me, baby?"

"Don't be silly. Would I be getting all riled up if I didn't like you? I like you a darn sight more than you like me," she added, pouting.

I patted her affectionately. "Why do you say that, sweetness?"

"Because you haven't been up to see me in more than three months," she reminded me.

I said: "You were too wrapped up in Jeff Fenwick. I didn't want to horn in."

"Oh, is that so? I wasn't the only one in his life. So why should he be the only one in mine? I'd have been glad to see you—any time!" she challenged me, swaying her hips a little. "Besides, poor Jeff's dead, now. You can be Number One boy any time you want, Dan!"

"That suits me," I said. I picked her up, carried her over to the divan on the other side of the room. I bounced her on the cushions, sank down next her.

She smiled and put her arms around me, pulled me against her ...

AFTER a while she said: "Okay, Mister Big. Now maybe you'll tell me what you really came here for."

"I want you to do me a favor," I said.

"*Now*, what?"

I chuckled. "I want you to play a role for me. Over at Altamount. Right away. Will you?"

"Tonight? Are you nuts?" she demanded. She looked puzzled.

I told her what was on my mind.

When I got through, she said: "Sure I will. Wait till I get dressed."

I watched her as she got ready to go. In detail, I can't tell you everything I saw, but it was worth watching. Just studying the grace with which she drew clear tan hose over her tapered legs; slid her feet into black pumps, was a liberal education. She wriggled herself into a black dress; dabbed herself with powder, lipstick. I absorbed quite a thump out of watching her. Every movement was poetry.

Pretty soon she said: "I'm all set. Let's ramble."

We went out.

I drove to Mayda Carman's joint next. Mayda was a tall, slender blonde with come-hither eyes, go-places curves. She didn't seem to like being rousted out of bed. But after a bit of palaver, she softened up; agreed to help me.

She got dressed, came down to my coupe with me.

Then I drove to Lola Lemoine's address. I struck a snag, there. Lola wasn't home. Her maid said: "She may not be back tonight, sir. I'm sorry."

I looked the maid over. She was a cute little trick. She had a turned-up nose, freckles, a nice little fig-ure. I said: "That's too bad. How would you like to earn ten seeds?"

She must have noticed the way my glance trav-eled over her scenery. She flushed, got sore. "What do you think I am, you big bum? Scram, before I...!"

I grinned. "Nix, baby. You got me all wrong. I want you to appear in a movie scene. Legitimate stuff."

She turned soft, quick.

"Oh-h-h—! Movies ...? Goodness! Why, y-yes! Wait until I get my coat—!"

Well, that completed my cast. I piled the Carman wren and Lola Lemoine's maid into my heap's rum-ble seat. Vio Yorkalle rode inside with me. I headed for the Altamount lot.

## CHAPTER X.
### The Scene Is Set

SOL LEVERING was already there. He had gathered a crew together on Sound Stage "A." He had two actors, a grip, and a cameraman.

The grip was already beginning to spray vaporized oil-fog over the set.

I said: "Hi, Sol. You're sure nobody knows about this?"

"Nobody but the people here," he said. "I followed your instructions to the letter."

I looked things over. Sol's two actors were in make-up. One wore a turned-down slouch hat, sloppy clothes. With his coat collar up, he'd pass as Louie Frizzati in a medium distance shot.

The other ham made a fairly good double for Jeffery Fenwick. He was wearing a costume identical to the one Fenwick had on when he was croaked.

I placed the slender Carman frail and Lola Lemoine's maid inside the window of the gloomy, deserted house. In the meantime, Vio Yorkalle hunted up a black wig, put it on. She smeared yellow grease-paint over her pan. That would register dead white on celluloid.

I told the cameraman exactly what I wanted him to do. He went after film; came back and threaded it into the blimp-covered camera on the nearest crane—the crane on which Foster Kinkaid had perched while filming Jeffery Fenwick's death-scene.

I said: "You're sure the camera will pick up a pistol-flash from up there, *no matter where it comes from?*"

"Sure. Can't miss. I'm using a wide angle lens. It

would register light even if it were right alongside me, here." He climbed down, pulled out a tape-measure, paced off his distances. He chalked the places where my actors were to stand.

Sol Levering touched my shoulder. "How about sound, Turner? You didn't tell me to bring a mixer. I'm no expert on mikes, myself."

I said: "Sound doesn't count, this time. We'll play it silent, like the old days. Now I want a list of every-body who was on this set tonight when Fenwick got rubbed out. Actors, actresses, extras, grips, juicers, carpenters, soundmen, cameramen—everybody. Can do?"

"Can do. Wait a minute." He toddled off to the executive building; came back about ten minutes later. "Here you are." He handed me a slip of paper.

I scanned it in a hurry. Jeffery Fenwick. Asta Valenska. Louie Frizzati. The two extra girls. Foster Kinkaid, director. Kinkaid's assistant. A scrip-clerk. Harry Treller, the cameraman. Three other lens-hounds. Four electricians. Five grips—property men and scene-shifters. Two sound-men; one on the set to handle the mikes and one upstairs in the mixing booth.

All in all, it made quite a roster. Twenty-three people, all told, had been on Sound Stage "A" at the time of the murder. Out of these twenty-three two weren't breathing any more. Jeffery Fenwick and Louie Frizzati.

I checked over the names, addresses. I turned back to Sol Levering. "You've got your properties arranged? You understand exactly how I want this thing shot?"

He said: "Maybe you'd better go over it again for me."

I talked fast for about four minutes. "Got it?" I wound up.

"Yes."

I said: "Good. As soon as you get the scene in the can, send everybody home. Tell them to keep their kissers padlocked. Then have a rush positive made. Be ready to show it in the biggest projection-room you've got. We'll have a hell of a sizable audience."

He looked at me. "Aren't you going to stay and watch me make this take?"

"No. I've got things to do, people to see. I'll be meeting you. When do you think you'll be ready?"

He looked at his wrist watch. "It's half-past two in the morning now. Give me, say, an hour and a half. I'll work fast. That will make it four A. M. Okay?"

I said: "Okay," and went out.

UP in one of the main buildings I located a phone. I dialed police headquarters. Dave Donaldson wasn't there. He'd gone home.

I rang his house. After a while he answered. "Donaldson talking. Who is it and why?"

I said: "Dan Turner. Listen. I've got a list of names

and addresses for you. Copy 'em down as I read 'em. Then round up everybody on the list. See that they're all on the Altamount lot by four o'clock. Use every copper in the department if you have to. But get 'em there!"

"Say, what is this?" he snarled. "Who the hell do you think you're giving orders to?"

I said: "To you, you lug. I'm going to hand you the murderer of Jeffery Fenwick, Louie Frizzati and Dolly Devorely. Or wouldn't you care for that?"

"Damn you, Turner!" he rasped. "I told you to keep your beak out óf this mess! I know who bumped Fenwick and those other two. It was the dame from Trenton. I've got the blast out for her. We'll catch her before she gets a chance to lam out of L. A. Go home and go to sleep. I'm sick of your meddling!"

I said: "Wait a moment. I've helped you plenty in the past, haven't I?"

"Yeah. So what? You loused up the detail on this job, and I don't mean maybe."

"Okay," I told him soothingly. "I'm making up for all my mistakes. You do what I ask. You won't be sorry."

He grumbled a while. Then he said: "Well, all right. But if this turns out to be another of your crackbrained, half-cocked duds, I'll—"

"Sure. I know. You'll jerk my tin. You'll take away my private detective's license. So okay. I'll run that risk. You have these people on the Altamount lot at four o'clock." I dictated the list to him.

When I got through he said: "Say—damn it! Those are the people who were on that sound stage with Fenwick—"

I said: "Yeah. Right you are again."

"But what about Foster Kinkaid and Asta Valenska and Harry Treller? You didn't mention them."

I said: "I'll bring that bunch myself. And I'll also have the Trenton frill with me."

"You *what?* Listen—do you know where she is?" he blew up.

"I'll have her with me at four o'clock," I said. "And by the way: two more things. Pick up a fat, one-eyed guy at the apartment house where Louie Frizzati lived. I don't like the color of his breath. He tried to maul me, earlier tonight. And send one of your official sedans to my stash, right away. With a cop to drive it. I won't be able to squeeze everybody into my coupe."

He snorted: "Wouldn't you sooner have a coach and four, Your Highness?"

I said: "Nuts," and rang off in his ear.

I went out, crawled into my buggy. I drove home.

The blonde cutie was waiting for me. "Mr. Turner—did you—"

I said: "Put these on, baby, and held her clothes out to her.

She looked surprised at the ice in my voice. She

took her torn dress, went into the bedroom. Then she came back out, slipped into her coat. "Are we g-going somewhere?"

I said: "Yeah. Stick out your hands."

She did. I hauled out my nippers, snicked them over her wrists.

"Wh-what—why—" she wailed. "H-handcuffs ...!"

I said: "Sure. Come on." I took her elbow, pulled her out of the apartment. We went downstairs. She was sobbing, away deep in her throat.

THERE was a black sedan at the curb. It had "L.A.P.D." lettered on it. It was a police department jalopy. A guy puffed out from behind the wheel. He was grinning at me.

I said: "Donaldson!"

"Sure. What did you expect, King Tut? I'm your chauffeur, wise guy. I'm going to see that you don't play any tricks—" Suddenly he spotted the yellow-haired baby behind me. He said: "Who the hell—?"

I said: "Lieutenant Donaldson, meet the lady from Trenton. The one who sent those threatening letters to Jeffery Fenwick."

The girl moaned: "You dirty double-crosser! And to think I t-trusted you...!"

Donaldson said: "Turner, I apologize. You've delivered me the killer, just like you said you would! Boy, you're okay!"

"Maybe. Maybe not," I clipped out. "Let's get going. Drive out to Crenshaw. We'll pick up Harry Treller first."

"What's the use of all that stuff, now?" Dave asked me. "The case is closed. I've got my prisoner."

I said: "Play it my way, Dave. Get started."

I sat in the back seat with the girl. Donaldson drove. The cutie stayed as far away from me as she could get. I didn't blame her much. She thought I was a heel. I probably was. But I wasn't running any chances.

Dave stopped in front of Treller's place. I managed to roust Harry out of bed after a while. I said: "Listen, Harry. I'm going to need you again. Will you go to the studio with me, like a good guy?"

He rubbed the sleep out of his lamps. "Sure. Wait until I climb into my shoes and pants."

Pretty soon he was dressed. He sat up front with Donaldson. I said: "The Gayboy Arms, Dave. On Wilshire. Foster Kincaid's apartment."

We went there. I left the others in the car; took the elevator up to Kinkaid's floor. I rang his bell.

After a long wait, Kinkaid himself opened up. I said: "Hi, Fos. I want—"

He said: "You lousy son of a ...!" and slugged me on the jaw.

## CHAPTER XI.
### The End of the Round-Up

**M**Y BRAINS rattled around inside my noggin. Lightning flashed in front of my peepers. Thunder roared in my ears. That was one of the sweetest belts I ever soaked up.

I went to my knees. Kinkaid leaped over me. He started down toward the elevators.

I shook my head, finally got it clear. I yanked out my roscoe. I yelled: "Freeze, Kinkaid—before I fill your kidneys full of lead!"

He froze.

I staggered toward him. "Thought you'd make a get-away, huh?"

He said: "Put down that gun and I'll beat the tripe out of you."

"No, thanks," I said. "Once was plenty. What was the idea, sloughing me that way? Guilty conscience?"

He got pale. "I don't know what you're talking about."

I said: "The hell you don't. You know I'm working on the Fenwick murder beef."

"Say, listen!" he snarled. "Are you accusing me of—"

"I'm not accusing you of anything—yet. I came up here to ask a favor. I want you to go down to the Altamount lot with me. But first I'd like to know why you used my kisser for a punching bag."

"Because I hate slimy double-crossers!" he rasped.

"Meaning me?" I said.

"Meaning you! You're tired of being a private snoop. You're looking for a soft berth in pictures. You thought you could gyp me out of my job, you yellow—"

I said: "Wait a second. What the hell are you getting at?"

"Don't play stupid, flatfoot. I've got a friend that's a grip at the studio. He phoned me a while ago; said you had talked Sol Levering into remaking that last scene of my new opus. You were trying to show me up. Trying to convince Levering you're a better director than I am."

I stared at him. He sounded sincere enough. And he had a rep for being a conceited fat-head. Maybe he really thought I'd been trying to cut his throat with Levering. But on the other hand, maybe it was just a stall. He used to be an actor before he started directing; he knew how to make a role look convincing. There was a chance he thought I was going to put the pinch on him. That might be why batted me, tried to take a powder.

I couldn't tell for sure. And I had no way of squeezing the real truth out of him. Not just then. There wasn't time. The only thing I could do was take him with me, along with the others, and see what happened.

I said: "Listen, Fos. You and I will fight this out some other day. Right now you're coming with me. If you try to make a break, I'll drill a hole in you to see if I can strike oil."

Then I edged him into the elevator, took him downstairs.

I LOADED him into the back seat of Donaldson's sedan, alongside the yellow-haired wren. I kept my roscoe against his ribs. I said: "Okay, Dave. Drive out to Asta Valenska's place."

We headed for Beverly. Donaldson didn't spare the horse-power, either. When he stopped, I said: "Keep everybody together, Dave. I'll be back in a minute."

I rang the Valenska bell. A maid let me in. I said: "I'll go up to Miss Valenska's room. You run along." I patted her, gave her a shove.

She hesitated. Then she said: "I remember you! You're a detective! You were here tonight, during all that shooting."

I said: "Yeah," and went upstairs. I walked into Asta's boudoir without knocking. I switched on the light.

It woke her up. She sat upright. The covers fell away from her. She was wearing sheer pajamas of black silk. White skin looks gorgeous through the lacework! She started to scream.

I put my arms around her shoulders. "Easy does it, sweetness. It's Dan Turner."

"Y-you—!"

"Yeah. I think I've landed Jeff's murderer. I need

your help. Let's see how fast you can get dressed."

She slipped out of bed. She turned her back to me, yanked her pajamas off. She forgot all about me. For a second I glimpsed a statue carved out of white marble. Then she slid a white Princess slip down over her curves. It settled, clung. It was like a curtain going down on a Follies tableau. She grabbed a dress, wriggled into it. Her bare feet burrowed into high-heeled slippers. She wrapped a coat around her. "I'm ready, Dan."

I said: "We'll use your car if you don't mind." Then I went downstairs ahead of her. I yelled: "Hey, Donaldson—go ahead. I'll follow in Miss Valenska's heap."

Dave's jalopy pulled away. Asta and I went around to her garage, climbed into her Rolls. I drove. We headed for the Altamount lot.

Asta sat close to me. "What's happening?"

I put my free arm around her waist. I said: "We've got the dame that threatened your husband. And I'm going to pull a fast one."

## CHAPTER XII.
### The Flash in the Fog

WE PARKED on the Altamount lot. I saw Donaldson taking Treller, Kinkaid, and the blonde cutie into the main building. I kept my arm around Asta's waist. I whispered:

"Don't be surprised at anything that happens. Keep your shirt on. Just watch close."

We walked inside.

Sol Levering was standing by a door. It led into a miniature theater. I stopped. I whispered: "Everything set, Sol?"

He nodded. He looked strained.

I led Asta to a seat. The room was plenty crowded. Cops lined the walls, guarded the exits. I counted heads. Everybody was there.

I walked up to the front; stood before the movie-screen. I said: "Attention, please."

The room got quiet.

I said: "You've all probably guessed why you're here. Each of you was on Sound Stage 'A' tonight when Jeffery Fenwick was murdered. You saw him killed—and yet you didn't see anything at all. On account of the artificial fog, the actual bump-off was hidden from everybody. Even the camera doesn't show what happened. All it got was shadows, movement. I'll let you look for yourself. You up there in the projection-booth—run off the reel for me, please."

The lights went out. I stepped aside. The screen glared with white brilliance, Then the movie began.

There was the thick, drifting fog. The deserted house. The two wrens at the lower window. Jeffery Fenwick walked on. The mists swallowed him. Then came movement, over to the left. A blurred stab of flame. Fenwick crumpling, falling.

The scene stopped suddenly. The screen got glaring white again. The house-lights came on.

I started talking some more. "You have just looked at a man dying. Actually dying," I said.

Somebody moaned, sobbed. It was Asta Valenska. I felt sorry for her.

But I had to go through with it now. I said: "You all know that shot was fired by Louie Frizzati. I mean the spurt of flame you just saw on the screen. But Frizzati's gun was loaded with blanks. He didn't kill Fenwick. In fact, Louie himself was bumped off, later tonight."

There came a lot of gasps. Plenty of guys in the audience hadn't yet heard about Frizzati and his moll being croaked. It was news to them.

I said: "Now, Frizzati was killed for a very good reason. He knew who had murdered Fenwick. Or anyhow, he had a good idea. He was about to spill his guts. He was shot to keep him from talking."

Somebody yelled at me: "If Frizzati was so damned innocent, why did he try to run away?"

It was Foster Kinkaid who snarled the question. I said: "That's easy. Louie had a police record. He knew he was in a jam. He had fired a blank at Fenwick. At the same instant, somebody else fired a real slug. Louie must have thought he'd be framed for the job. He got scared, took a powder. Then later, when I caught up with him, he started to tell me what he knew. He wanted to clear himself. He was cooled off before he could talk."

I STOPPED long enough for that to sink in. Then I went on: "It's perfectly clear that Jeffery Fenwick was burned down by somebody on the sound stage—somebody on the set or hiding beyond the camera lines. The fake fog was a swell cloak. Even the film didn't pick up the flame-streak from the actual death-gun. The fog was too thick."

Harry Treller called out: "If that's the case, what's this all about? What are you trying to prove, Turner?"

I said: "I'm going to prove plenty. The killer didn't figure on something that happened by accident; something that was to give the game dead away.

"Let's go back a minute. Jeffery Fenwick had been getting certain threatening letters. His past had caught up with him. We won't go into that. But the murderer knew he was getting these threats. So it looked like a swell chance to bump him—and blame it on the person who wrote the letters.

"Okay. Now for the important part. Have you ever heard of infra-red film? Sure. It's treated with special emulsion; sensitized to infra-red rays. The so-called 'dark rays'—invisible light.

"Infra-red film penetrates darkness, murk. When we had that cold spell here in California, the orange-growers saved their orchards by burning smudge-pots for heat. The smoke settled over Hollywood like a blanket. But most picture companies went right ahead with their shooting schedules. Location units weren't affected. Because they used infra-red film. It cuts right through smoke.

"Now, here's the twist. When Jeffery Fenwick's last scene was shot tonight, a mistake had been made. By accident, one of the cameras got loaded with the wrong kind of film. *Infra-red film!* You didn't know that, Kinkaid. Neither did you, Treller. Nobody knew it. The camera also had a wide-angle lens. And now I'm going to show you who killed Fenwick.—Okay, projection-room. *Roll 'em!*"

The lights went out. The screen came to life.

I could see the rolling veil of fake fog. But I could also see through it. There stood Jeffery Fenwick, facing away from the lens. In the background, the two extra girls showed at the window. Over to the left stood Louie Frizzati and Asta Valenska.

Frizzati raised his roscoe. Flame belched out of it. Then, right alongside of him, there was another streak of light. *It vomited out of Asta Valenska's handbag!*

I heard a shriek. The picture stopped. Somebody forgot to turn the house-lights back on. Asta Valenska yelled: "God damn you—"

Hell broke loose. Harry Treller's voice sliced through the blackness. "I killed Fenwick! Come on, Asta—quick—"

A roscoe went: *"Chow-chow!"* I went plunging up the aisle. People got in my way. I lashed out with my dukes. I punched a path for myself. I roared: "Dave! Dave Donaldson! Grab Asta Valenska—"

THE lights came on. Asta was trying to reach the back exit. She had a smoking gat in her mitt. Harry Treller was sprawled in the aisle. Blood was gushing out of his kisser.

I dived at the Valenska bimbo. She went down. She tried to twist her gat around; tried to plug me. I bopped her on the jaw.

I said: "The jig's up, baby. You were crazy jealous of Jeff Fenwick. He wasn't true to you. He wasn't built that way. He was a lady-killer. The dames fell for him in droves. He never learned to keep away from them, even after he married you. He had a regular Hollywood harem."

"Yes! A harem—that's what he had! Damn him—"

I said: "You knew he was chasing. You also knew he was being threatened by some girl back east. He had ruined the girl's sister; she killed herself. So you decided to bump Jeff for his catting around. You planned to blame it on the girl who wrote the letters.

"You shot him on the set tonight. The gun was in your handbag. The handbag choked the flame-flash. But Louie Frizzati knew you were the one.

"That's why you tried to steer me away from Louie. You were afraid I'd find him, get the truth out of him. So you paid me a grand ... among other things ... to lay off him and hunt for the girl who wrote the letters.

"That's what tipped me off. Why were you so anxious to clear Louie Frizzati? You fronted for him because you were scared he'd give you away. You even traced him to his moll's cottage. You got there in time to hear him start spilling his guts to me. So you drilled him—and his girl-friend."

She said: "You rat! I'd have got away with it if you hadn't found that infra-red film—"

I said: "Well, now that you've confessed, I'll tell you something. That was a fake roll. Sol Levering made it for me, tonight. With a substitute cast. I did-n't have any real evidence against you. But I was sure you were the killer. The film was a trap. You didn't see yourself on the screen just now. That was Vio Yorkalle, acting your part—*and doing it the way you actually did it!* It got a confession out of you, baby. That's what counts!"

Dave Donaldson leaned over me. He grated: "Harry Treller's dead. Asta plugged him. Why the hell did she—?"

I said: "Harry loved Asta. He was her sweetie be-fore she fell for Fenwick. He told me he'd go to hell for her. That's what he was willing to do, just now. He was willing to take a murder rap for her. But when he tried to drag her out of here, she lost her head. She pulled her gat, let him have it."

Dave said: "That makes four bump-offs." He snagged a pair of nippers over Asta's wrists, yanked her to her feet. He said: "Too damned bad we can't hang you four times!"

Her crimson lips writhed. "Once will be enough, copper!" she whispered dully.

## CHAPTER XIII.
### Blonde Bait

I ANKLED back to where the blonde Trenton cutie was hunched down in a chair. I unlocked her bracelets. I said: "Sorry I had to put you through the wringer this way, kiddo. But I had to. Otherwise Donaldson wouldn't have worked with me, helped me pull the trap on the Valenska bimbo. My movie stunt was the bait for Valenska. But you were the bait for Donaldson. Blonde bait. Blonde justice."

She looked at me. "I—I understand . . . Dan . . ." she whispered.

I said: "How about a little snort of Vat 69 to calm your nerves, baby? I've got a fresh fifth in my apartment."

"I—I like your apartment ...!" she smiled at me.

We went out into the open air. The sun was just coming up. The morning looked fresh, rosy. Pretty soon it would be breakfast-time for most people.

# DEATH'S BLUE DISCS

Dan Turner could see no other way out. He must take the law in his own hands; but he figured it was worth the risk if it would get Judy Prescott out of the jam she was in

SOMETIMES a guy has to take the law in his own hands—and this was one of the times. It was early evening when I anchored my jalopy near the isolated bungalow in Laurel Canyon, switched off my head lamps, and made sure my .32 roscoe was easy in its shoulder rig. Not that I expected to do any blasting; but you never can tell what might happen when you're running the brand of bluff I was about to pull.

Alongside me, Judy Prescott shivered and said: "Mr. Turner—Dan—you'll be c-careful, won't you? I wouldn't want you to get in trouble on my account ..."

"Sure I'll be careful," I said. "I've been a private dick in Hollywood too many years to be caught with my slacks at half staff. Besides, you're paying me a fee for this job. And I'm accustomed to running risks. You quit worrying and wait here for me; I won't be gone long."

She shivered again; I could feel her warm figure trembling against me, and I got a copious bang out of the contact. Judy was a nifty little brunette dish, all cuddlesome contours and come-hither curves— especially where her fuzzy Angora sweater was stretched taut by firm, pulsating mounds. In contrast to the blackness of her hair, her piquant puss looked pale, wan. That was to be expected, considering the pickle she was in. Her career as a singing star in Stormer Productions, her entire cinema future, depended on my success during the next few minutes.

I started to clamber out of my bucket, aim myself toward the bungalow ahead. A blackmailer

*The bullet came from the bedroom doorway.*

calling herself Trix Warren hung out in that stash—
and I was about to lower the boom on her. But first I
hesitated long enough to say: "You're certain this is
the address, Judy?"

"Yes. It's wh-where she told me to bring the
money."

I scowled. "When this Warren female phoned

you, she claimed she had two master discs—phonograph recordings—that you made for a clandestine platter company about a year ago. Right?"

Judy nodded forlornly. She looked so damned woeful I felt like grabbing her in my arms, soothing her with kisses. She was the sort of wren that arouses a man's protective instincts. But I restrained my wayward impulses, kept my mitts to myself. I said: "At the time you waxed these ditties twelve months ago, you were an extra girl struggling to keep beans on the table for yourself and your kid sister, Kitty. The going was tough; you jumped at the chance to sing a couple of numbers for fifty seeds apiece. That much dough looked important to you."

"I w-was broke ..."

"But it was dirty geetus," I said. "The songs were bluer than hell. If you hadn't been so hard up you wouldn't have sung them."

"Oh-h-h, no!"

I SAID: "A week after you warbled this risque stuff you got your big break. Lew Stormer, the shoestring producer, hired you for a minor role in a musical quickie. You clicked. Stormer gave you a starring contract at a steady increase in salary until now you're dragging down three grand a week. Which is tops for an independent outfit like Stormer's."

She nodded.

"Out of your first decent paycheck," I summed

up, "you bought back the blue records you'd made; suppressed them. You were told the master discs had been destroyed. But now this Trix Warren dame—a person you've never even met—is trying to shake you down. She says she has those master records and threatens to release them to the Hays office unless you pay her fifty grand."

"And I haven't g-got that much!" Judy whimpered. "But if those songs are made public they'll ruin me ..."

"They won't be made public," I said. "I'll get them back if I have to jerk somebody apart." Then I ankled away from the car.

I reached the house, thumbed the bell. Nobody answered—which seemed damned screwy because I could see lights inside. On a hunch I tried the door, found it unlatched. I barged into the living room and felt my glims suddenly popping. I gasped: "What the hell!"

The room was a mess. Chairs were overturned; books and papers were scattered to hellangone. Near an upset table lay a red-haired, voluptuous jane in ripped silk pajamas. The top of her noggin was blown open; blood and sticky brains made a puddle under her. She looked deader than a fried trout.

I didn't bother to fumble for her pulse. I could see it was useless. Besides, I had my eye on another sprawled figure across the room; a feminine figure huddled in a limp heap. The instant I glued the focus on her, I tabbed her. She was Judy Prescott's kid sister, Kitty.

Kitty's golden hair was in tumbled disarray; her dress was torn to strips as if in some terrific battle. I could see the snowy curves through a wisp of ruined bandeau; her stems were slender and shapely in laddered chiffon where the hem of her skirt had ridden northward beyond her knees. I catapulted toward her, leaned over, jammed my palm against the resilient region of her heart.

I drew a deep breath of relief when I found her ticker was beating. She wasn't croaked; merely unconscious. I rolled her over, looked for possible wounds. I didn't find any. All I saw was sleek, velvety skin and a lot of enticing allurements.

BUT I didn't have time to enjoy the scenery. There were other things on my mind. Near Kitty's right hand there was a .28 Belgian automatic that smelled of burned powder when I sniffed its muzzle. And clenched in her dainty left duke were two busted wax phonograph discs.

That spelled plenty to me. The dame whose dome was blown open must have been the blackmailer, Trix Warren. And the shattered platters in Kitty's grasp were obviously the two master records of the blue ditties Judy Prescott had warbled a year ago.

It all added up to make grim sense. Evidently

Kitty had found out her older sister was being shaken down and had come here to swipe the off-color discs. The Warren jane must have surprised her, tried to stop her. There had been a fracas. In self-defense, Kitty Prescott had drilled the red-haired bimbo and then fainted.

Well, according to my notion, the Trix Warren she-louse had got what she deserved. And I couldn't bring myself to let Kitty face a murder beef for a kill that struck me as entirely justifiable. Sure, I'm a private snoop with a badge and a license; I'm sworn to uphold the laws and statutes. But this was different. Judy Prescott's sister deserved a break and I made up my mind to give it to her.

I grabbed the record-fragments and the Belgian roscoe; pocketed them. I took a swivel around the room to make sure there weren't any other clues. Then I lifted Kitty in my arms, lugged her out of the bungalow toward my parked heap. She was a sweet burden. I drew a thump out of carrying her.

JUDY PRESCOTT bounced out of my coupe like a brunette bombshell when she saw me coming. "It— it's Kitty!" she gasped. "My God — what happened?"

I said: "Cork it, kiddo. We've got to get her home before hell froths over. Get behind that wheel and drive. Soup this bucket!"

She kicked the starter. I climbed in alongside her, held Kitty on my lap. My fingers accidentally sank into pliant softness as I supported the blonde doll. The sensation was damned nice.

Judy headed for her modest two-story tepee this side of Westwood Village. Presently we reached the shebang. There was a maroon sedan parked in the driveway. A guy got out of the sedan, came toward us. "Judy!" he said.

I recognized him as Judy flew into his arms. He was her fiance, Art Melville, a script writer for Alta-mount and a hell of a good egg. A look of bewilder-ment came over his handsome pan when he stared over Judy's shoulder and saw me toting Kitty out of my jalopy. He said: "Dan Turner! What the devil goes on?"

"Tell you later," I grunted. "Open the door, Judy."

She did. I carried her unconscious sister inside and upstairs to a boudoir. Art Melville and Judy fol-lowed me. But before they could say anything the doorbell rang downstairs.

I felt my gullet tightening. Maybe the cops had caught hep to the Laurel Canyon kill, I thought. Maybe they'd followed my chariot and were about to make a pinch. I said: "Quick, Judy—go down and see who it is. You too, Art."

They pelted down the steps. I watched over the banister; saw Judy opening the portal. But it wasn't a cop who ankled in. It was a dwarfish slug with an eagle-beak beezer and soft, gentle glims. Judy said: "Why, h-hello, Mr. Stormer ..."

I breathed easier when I knew who her visitor was. Lew Stormer ran the studio where Judy Prescott starred; there wasn't an ounce of harm in him. I went back to Kitty's boudoir.

*"It's Kitty!" she gasped. "What happened?"*

She was still senseless. I began rubbing her temples, chafing her wrists. Presently her long golden lashes fluttered. She stared up at me. She cringed.

"Please—no—d-don't arrest me!" she whimpered.

Then she twined her arms around my neck, spooned me an unexpected kiss that sent live steam sizzling past my tonsils. "I d-don't w-want to go to j-jail—!"

She clung to me, welded her delectable form to my chest; her lips were hot and parted and succulent on my kisser. I felt my temperature coming up; after all, I'm as human as the next slob. But I pushed her back and said: "Look, sweet stuff. You needn't be scared. I'm not going to put the nab on you for croaking that Warren broad."

Her peepers widened open. "Y-you aren't going to arrest me? Even though you know I k-killed her?"

"You were trying to save Judy's career," I said. "That rates a medal in my book. If I've got anything to say about it, you won't even come under suspicion. Now give your nerves a nap. They need it." I blew her a kiss; left her.

WHEN I ankled downstairs, Judy was waiting for me in the hall. "Dan!" she whispered. "What's wrong with Kitty? What happened in that bungalow? You've got to tell me!"

I set fire to a gasper. Then I spilled the whole works. It seemed the best thing to do.

When I finished, Judy's pan was sallow around the fringes. "Kitty ... a murderer? My God ... this ruins everything!" she moaned.

I said: "How come?"

"Lew Stormer's waiting in the library to see her. He—he promised Kitty a role in my next picture; she could have had a chance to make a star of herself the same as I've done. But now ..."

I said: "Hold tight, Judy. If Stormer wants to give your sister a break in pictures, let him. Nobody's going to know anything about what happened tonight in Laurel Canyon. I'll cover for you. You can trust me."

"You m-mean ...?"

"I mean I'm going to keep Kitty's name out of it; yours too."

Her dark eyes glistened. "You're s-swell, Dan!" she whispered; and she came close to me, gave me a quick kiss of gratitude.

I said: "Forget it. Make an excuse to get rid of Lew Stormer until Kitty's had time to calm down. Meanwhile I'm going back to that bungalow to make sure I didn't leave any loose clues." Then I barged out to my heap, aimed it toward Laurel Canyon.

It seemed funny as hell for me to be covering a murder; the idea pinched bruises on my conscience until I considered how much Kitty Prescott deserved the help I was giving her. That made me feel a lot better. I braked my bucket to a stop about a block away from the death-bungalow; got out.

Then I froze. Somebody was coming out of that cottage. A dame.

LIGHT from inside the joint bathed her puss as she closed the front door after her. I recognized her. She was Loline Meade, a bit-player. I'd been on parties with her in the old days, knew her pretty damned well. But what the hell had she been doing in that house? And why was she leaving it so calmly when she couldn't have helped seeing the Warren woman's corpse in the living room? Any ordinary wren would have dashed out of that tepee with the shrieking meanies; but Loline Meade looked as passive as a cold storage oyster.

I started after her. But before I took three steps a maroon sedan drove up behind my jalopy. Somebody said: "Just a minute, shamus."

I pivoted; saw a guy coming toward me. He was Art Melville—Judy Prescott's fiance. "What the hell are *you* doing here?" I asked him.

He said: "I'm doing this," and slugged me on the whiskers. I wasn't expecting it; didn't have time to get set. His knuckles erupted against my chin, rocked my noggin back. I swayed like a drunk. He measured me, corked me again. I felt myself toppling. Then I didn't feel anything at all. I went bye-bye.

When I woke up, Melville and his maroon sedan were gone. And by that time there was no trace of Loline Meade, the quail who had barged so calmly out of the murder-cottage. I was all alone in the gloom.

I staggered upright, tried to shake away the bee-hive questions that buzzed in my think-tank. In the first place, why had Loline Meade been in that house? What, if anything, had she done about the murdered dame? And finally, why had Art Melville tailed me here to Laurel Canyon and put the slugs to me?

Maybe I'd find the answers inside the bungalow, I thought. So I stumbled toward the stash, opened the front door, walked in. Then I gasped: "What the hell!"

THERE wasn't any corpse in the living room. It had vanished. For a minute I thought maybe I was punch-drunk. Regardless of gender, defunct black-mailers can't get up and walk away from the scene of their demise. Yet the red-haired Trix Warren's car-cass was definitely absent.

It was fantastic as hell. I knew Loline Meade couldn't have glommed Trix Warren's remainders; all she'd carried out of the house was a thing that looked like an overnight bag. Then I considered Art Melville. Could he have made off with the corpse in his maroon sedan while I was listening to the bird-ies? Was that the reason he had knocked me coo-coo?

At least it was a theory. Perhaps he had wanted to dispose of the corpus delicti in order to shield Kitty Prescott, his future sister-in-law. But that didn't explain why he had bashed me. And I still couldn't savvy where that bit-player, Loline Meade, meshed into the picture.

Out of habit, I made a blurry frisk of the bungalow. The only thing I located to indicate a murder had ever been committed in the joint was a gooey mess of brains in a garbage can under the kitchen sink. When I saw it, I almost tossed my cookies. It reminded me of the way the Warren she-male had looked in death—with her skull blown open and her grey matter leaking out.

As things stacked up, it appeared that some maniac had performed a cerebral autopsy on the dead dame. But who? And why? It couldn't have been the cops; there was no indication that the law had been smelling around. Besides, police medical examiners don't usually leave a victim's parts in a garbage can...

I took another gander; did some fast thinking. An idea swatted me. I said: "By God! I wonder—!" and dashed out to my pile of iron; headed back toward Westwood.

I reached Judy Prescott's wikiup, rang her bell. She looked like a ghost when she let me in; her dark peepers seemed harried, haunted. "Dan!" she whispered. "Thank God you came back!"

I pinned the focus on her. "Has something gone haywire?"

"Y-yes." She poked an envelope at me. "This j-just came by special messenger. Open it. Look at it."

I flipped the flap, dug out a typewritten note and two candid camera prints. The pictures hit me like a punch in the teeth. They were flashbulb snaps of an interior room; the living room of that Laurel Canyon bungalow. The first one showed Kitty Prescott aiming a roscoe at Trix Warren, triggering a slub at her. You could see the flame-streak belching out of the muzzle like a thin tongue. The second print showed the Warren broad falling forward with her cranium blasted open. Kitty was standing to one side, watching her go down.

Judy moaned: "Read the n-note..."

I did. It said:

*"Miss Judith Prescott*

*The enclosed snaps will prove my thorough knowledge of your sister's crime. I was on hand when she committed murder and I took these pictures for proof in case of need. I might add that I have hidden the dead woman's body where I can easily lead the police to it if necessary. But you need have no fear if you act sensibly. All I ask is two-thirds of your weekly salary from now on. Later you will be told how to make the payments; and if you miss a single one, these pictures will be handed to the authorities along with the whereabouts of the corpse.*

*Signed, THE EYE."*

Judy took the note back when I finished scanning

it. She sobbed: "I'll have to p-pay—and go on pay-ing! I can't put Kitty in danger of arrest when she was only t-trying to help me ...!"

"No, you can't," I admitted. "It looks as if this is going to cost you two grand a week; maybe more if Lew Stormer boosts your wages." Then I took her hands, held them. I said: "Look, hon. Would you be willing to have me get you out from under this mess—even though it might mean putting the finger on someone you love?"

She stared at me. Her lips thinned. "You d-don't mean—?" Then her voice firmed. "For Kitty's sake, my answer is yes. I want you to—to do whatever should be done!"

THAT was the answer I wanted. I went back outside; headed for downtown Hollywood. After a while I gumshoed into a second-rate apartment building; walked up to the third floor. I tapped on the door of Loline Meade's flat.

Loline was wearing a sheer nightie and a frilly negligee when she opened up. Soft light came from within the room; silhouetted her lush curves. I could see the swelling sweep of her hips, the tapered dain-tiness of her gams, the bold hillocks of her breast through gossamer chiffon. She looked delicious. She also looked damned startled when she tabbed me.

"Wh-why, hello, Hawkshaw!" she said. "What on earth brings you here? I haven't seen you in ages!"

"You aren't going to arrest me?" she pleaded.

I followed her to a divan, pulled her down beside me. "I get around eventually," I grinned. "How's your private stock these days?"

"Some Vat 69 in the cellarette. I'll get you a snort." She undulated across the room, came back and handed me a tipple of my favorite juice. She poured herself one, raised it. "To old times."

I downed my slug and said: "No. To crime." I made my voice carry a double meaning.

"Crime?" she said. Some of the pink drained out

of her puss. "You're always talking business. Why not relax?" Then she nestled close to me and wriggled my arm around her waist.

Her nearness was damned pleasant. I decided on a system of shock treatment: maybe I could scare her into spilling what I wanted to know if I spread some oil before I cracked down. So I tightened my embrace. I tilted her chin back, glued a kiss on her moist lips. Her tongue fluttered on an indrawn breath: "M-m-m! You still know how, don't you?"

I said: "Instinct, babe," and ran a mitt over her shoulder.

The negligee pulled half open. "Instinct? You mean practise!" she giggled. But she didn't try to close the kimono.

I jammed her backward; pinned her. "Too bad you won't get any of it in prison," I rasped.

She stiffened. "P-prison—?"

"You heard me. There's a nice cell waiting for you up at Tehachapi, kiddo. You'll be in it for a hell of a long stretch."

"Wh-what do you mean? Let me up!" She squirmed, tried to get away from me.

I slipped her across the map. My fingers left red marks on her pallor. I said: "The joke's over, kiddo. I saw you leaving that Laurel Canyon bungalow tonight. I know all about the Trix Warren deal, and those candid snaps. Blackmailing is a penitentiary rap in this state—or didn't you know?"

"You—you wouldn't send me up!"

"The hell I wouldn't. Unless you come clean with me right now."

She put her arms around me, tried to pull me against her. "Please—don't make me t-tell! I c-can't! I'll be ... nice to you ... if you'll let me alone ..."

I said: "Ixnay. I want the whole story about what happened in Laurel Canyon. Otherwise you're going to the gow."

"I can't tell you! I d-don 't dare!"

"Take your choice," I said. "It's up to you. If you go on fronting for this other party, you'll do it behind bars."

Her mouth opened; words started to blurt. Then she stared beyond me. Her glims got glassy with terror. "No—oh, my God—don't shoot—!" she shrilled.

I tried to spring upright. Her grasp tangled me. From the bedroom doorway a roscoe yammered: "Ka-chow! Chow!" and I felt a sledgehammer nipping my noggin. Blackness exploded in waves through my nooks and crannies. I slumped forward; passed out.

I WOKE up with a corpse under me. Loline Meade's corpse. A slug had tunneled through her forehead, sent her to glory. My own head throbbed like a toothache where that second bullet had creased me. Only a cargo of typical Turner luck had kept me from being meat for the undertaker.

I swayed off the davenport, stood up. My knees quivered like overcooked spaghetti and there was blood on my temple; my own gore. It was sticky, thick, starting to congeal. That told me I'd been unconscious quite a while.

I yanked out my roscoe. It was a futile gesture; I knew it even before I frisked the flat. Whoever had shot Loline was long gone. The killer had lammed after triggering those two pills; had powdered under the impression that I'd been creamed along with the Meade jessie.

But that was a hell of a big mistake. I was alive— and I was thirsty for a damned big drink of vengeance. I made for the phone on the other side of the room; dialed Judy Prescott's number.

Judy answered in person. I said: "Hi, toots. Dan Turner calling. You alone?"

"No-no," her answer seemed guarded. "Art Melville is here with me. He came just a little while ago ..." I could tell from her tone that she wasn't exactly pleased.

"And Kitty?" I said.

"In the library talking to Lew Stormer about her part in my new picture," Judy said. "Wh-why?"

I said: "You'll find out," and rang off. I twirled the dial again; got a connection with police headquarters and asked for my friend Dave Donaldson of the homicide squad.

His voice rasped over the wire. "Lieutenant

Donaldson."

I said: "This is Turner. I've got a nice fresh kill for you. A cutie named Loline Meade. I almost got a dose of the same gun-poison myself," I tacked on grimly.

Dave let out a bellowing yelp. "Great Gahd! Where are you? How did it happen and why? Who did it?"

I said: "Meet me in Westrood right away and I'll dish out all the answers." I gave him Judy Prescott's address, told him to make it snappy. Then I hung up, whirled, heaved my heft out of the apartment. I went down to my leaping Lena and goosed the tripes out of it.

MY brakes showered sparks in front of the Prescott tepee just as Donaldson's official police-department sedan came up behind me. He lumbered out of his equipage; lunged toward me. He said: "Okay, brain-guy. Let's have it."

"Hold your toupee on," I said. "And keep your hog-leg handy. I think we're about to make a pinch." I led him to Judy's front door; fingered the jingle-button.

Judy opened up, I grabbed her by the hand, hauled her toward the library. Kitty Prescott and Lew Stormer and Art Melville stared at me as I barged in. The shrimp-sized producer got a bewildered look in his gentle glims; the blonde Kitty turned pale around the borders when she spotted Donaldson and his badge. And then Art Melville's eyebrows pulled together in a thundercloud scowl. "Get your hands off Judy!" he snarled. He moved toward me.

I said: "Pipe down with the jealousy stuff. I'm about to put the arm on a killer."

The instant the words were out of my kisser, Judy Prescott went nuts. "Damn you for a double crossing louse!" she screeched. "You promised you wouldn't tell—!" Then she clawed at me with her fingernails like a brunette wildcat.

I hated to slug her, but I had to. I made a loose fist and popped her on the dimple. She flew backward, landed in an overstuffed easy chair. Her skirt flurried upward to her thighs; pink step-ins winked coyly against creamy flesh ...

Art Melville said: "You stinking son!" and picked up a brass book-end, tried to beam me with it. Little Lew Stormer grabbed his arm, stopped him. Then Melville shook off the undersized studio executive, tried to get at me again. But he froze when he saw Dave Donaldson's service .38 making faces at him.

I said: "Okay, everybody. Quiet down. This is a murder beef."

"It is not!" Kitty Prescott yowled. "You're haywire if you think—"

I tossed a grin at the blonde doll. "Thanks for admitting it," I said. "You're right. There was no murder committed in Laurel Canyon tonight. But there was a genuine rub-out in Loline Meade's stash. *Lew Stormer, you're under arrest for croaking Loline.*"

The diminutive movie mogul blew his topper. His eaglebeak nostrils widened; his eyes got full of hellfire. "You'll never pin it on me!" he yeeped. And he drew a heater; triggered a slug at me.

But his shot went wild—because Dave Donaldson fired first. Dave sent a .38 cannonball through Stormer's skinny chest. The impact smashed the producer back against the wall, pinned him there for a second. Then the little bozo slumped, fell, started coughing up red froth. "God ... God ...!" he moaned.

I STOOD over him and said: "Too bad, mister. You wanted to save a few grand—and now you're paying with your life."

His glims glared into mine; his kisser formed voiceless curses.

I said: "There never were any master records of Judy Prescott's blue songs. When she bought back those records a long while ago, the original discs were destroyed by the company that had made them.

"But you found out that they had once existed; and you schemed up a blackmail stunt. Judy was your top star; in fact, your only star. Until you got her under contract you were nothing but a shoe-string operator on Poverty Row. Judy's success pulled your quickie company into the upper brackets.

"She was worth plenty of lettuce; yet all you paid her was three thousand clams a week. Buttons. And even then you weren't satisfied. You wanted to save two-thirds of that sum; wanted her services for a lousy grand."

Stormer choked another oath.

I said: "You worked through Judy's kid sister. Kitty was envious of Judy's screen success; wanted to be a star in her own right. You promised her a chance if she'd play ball—and she fell for it. You started by basing a fake shake-down on certain phonograph discs that didn't exist.

"The next step was for Kitty to pretend she'd killed the blackmailer. That murder was phoney; was staged only so you could take snapshots showing Kitty as a murderess. You knew Judy would pay any sum to keep the kid out of prison."

Judy turned, stared at her shivering blonde sister. "You—you were in the scheme to blackmail me? Oh-h-h, Kitty ...!"

I kept on talking to Stormer. I said: "There never was a jane named Trix Warren. All you did was to rent that Laurel Canyon bungalow and hire a bit-player named Loline Meade to play the role of corpse. Loline wore a red wig and false top-skull over her real noggin. That was a simple makeup trick. Inside the top-skull you placed a calf-brain from some butcher shop. Then you chopped the whole thing open; it gave the appearance of a wren with her head busted by a bullet."

"You ... think you're ... smart ...!" Stormer gasped.

I said: "Smart enough to recognize a calf-brain when I saw it in that garbage can. That was my tip-off. I knew the Laurel Canyon kill was a fake. And I asked myself who could possibly benefit.

"Then when Judy showed me the blackmail letter she had received, I had my answer. I realized Kitty was a part of the phony murder; she'd posed willingly for the fake snapshots. But there had to be a third party in the setup; someone who'd snapped the pix.

"That third party was you, Lew Stormer. You'd offered Kitty a movie job; that was her motivation. And your own motive was a desire to save two-thirds of the salary you were paying Judy."

He coughed again; the sound rattled in his perforated lungs. "I wish ... I'd killed you ... when I ... had the chance ...!" he wheezed.

I SAID: "You tried to. That was in Loline Meade's joint. You must have been in her boudoir when I called on her. Maybe you were paying her off for enacting the role of corpse in Laurel Canyon. But when I began to put the pressure on her, you got scared. You were afraid she'd spill the beans, implicate you. A blackmail rap would wreck you and your producing company. You'd lose Judy Prescott, your one big money-maker.

"So you took the obvious way out. You croaked Loline Meade to keep her from talking. You tried to cool me, too—but you missed. And now you're washed up."

He was more than washed up. He was dead. I don't think he even heard my final summing-up. He had already stopped breathing.

Art Melville strode toward me, awkwardly. "Listen, Dan. I hope you don't think I was mixed up in it," he said.

"Sure not," I told him. "You slugged me because you'd seen Judy giving me a grateful kiss—and you were jealous. Forget it."

I stuck out my mitt. He shook it. Then I heard a whimpering sound behind me. I turned; saw that Kitty Prescott had got down on her knees in front of Judy. "Sis ... please ... don't have me arrested! I—I'm sorry I let Stormer talk me into the blackmail thing ... and I didn't have anything to do with murder! Oh-h-h ... won't you forgive me ...?"

If I had been Judy Prescott I'd have kicked that two-timing blonde doll square in the smeller. But Judy lifted Kitty, put her arms around her. "I forgive you."

# CRIMSON COMEDY

Dan never liked to poke around in other people's business, but this was once when he forgot his good resolutions. He started out to save a man from a beating and found himself involved in a series of the most brutal killings of his career

THEY wore masks made from handkerchiefs; they were four to one; and they were lambasting hell out of the little fat guy in the baggy tweeds. Nobody likes to watch a good fracas more than I do, but this was different. The odds were all wrong.

I copped an accidental gander at the brawl as I drove past Altamount Alley on my way home from a midnight preview. Even before I ruddered my bucket to the curb I could hear the fat guy 's moans, the dull thwack of fists kissing him on the features. The more he pleaded for mercy, the more those four blisters lowered the boom on him.

As a rule, I don't like to poke my smeller in somebody else's personal business. Not without an invitation in the form of a cash retainer, anyhow. I've got enough enemies in Hollywood already, the same as any other private hawkshaw. But when I piped the terrific lacing those vermin were dishing out to the corpulent slob, I forgot my good resolutions. Especially when he went down and they began kicking him in the belly.

I cut my ignition, catapulted out of my jalopy and sprinted hellity-larrup toward the center of the festivities. Like a narrow black notch, the alley separated Altamount Studios from the back lot of Super Pix next door. The only light came from a red bulb over an emergency fire exit far to the rear, just beyond where the trouble was taking place. And in the scarlet glow I saw I hadn't arrived any too damned soon.

The fat guy had quit struggling, quit trying to protect himself. He just quivered on the ground, a shapeless blob absorbing copious portions of shoeleather. "Please, boys . . ." he kept whimpering. "I'll pay Shanghai ... I swear to God..."

But the four plug-uglies weren't listening to him. And they were so interested in their football practice that they didn't hear me coming. Which was a break for me. I goosed more speed out of my gams and yodeled: "Belay it, you louse-bound scum!" Then I belted the nearest rodent full in the mush.

*"Lay off," I rasped, "before I start spraying poison from this Flit gun."*

I PACK a hundred and ninety pounds of solid heft on my six-feet-plus, and I poured every ounce of it into that roundhouse wallop; felt the satisfying jolt of it traveling up my arm. It was like smacking a ripe

canteloupe with an axe. The masked guy's noggin
rocked back and a blurt of katchup spewed from his
ruined kisser. He folded over, dripping teeth.

His three pals emitted an assortment of startled
language, laid off booting the fat bozo and sailed at
me. One of them dropped a blackjack out of his
sleeve, tried to mace me over the conk with it. He
swung like a gate.

I took the blow on my shoulder. It hurt to beat
hell. Then it went numb. I growled: "You asked for
this, cousin," and buried my left duke south of his
equator. Sure it was foul; you don't stop to consider
Marquis of Queensbury rules when some sharp apple is trying to cave in your roof with a blunt instrument.

My punch ripped a yowl of agony out of him. He
doubled up, holding himself. I pivoted to face the
remaining pair. One of them nipped me a lucky
poke on the button. Sparks erupted in front of my
glims. I gave ground, fought for balance. Another
bunch of fives tagged me. I felt my knees go rub-
bery.

I didn't dare take a count, though. I knew what
would happen if I did. Those masked hombres
would stomp on me until my kidneys whistled Old
Black Joe. So I bought myself a breathing spell by
tapping a trickle of claret out of the nearest trumpet.
Then I dug for the short-barreled .32 automatic I
always tote in a shoulder holster in case of necessity.

The way it turned out, I didn't need the rod after all. Yanking my coat open displayed the private tin-ware pinned to my vest. The guy with the leaking smeller panted: "Gawd, a copper! Let's get to hell out of here!" Then he and his chum took it on the lam, fast. The last I saw of them they were pelting out of the alley into the street with their hip pockets dipping sand.

The two they had left behind were stretched out cold; needed vulcanizing. But they could wait. The fat slug in the baggy tweeds came first.

He was flopping around on all fours, trying to shove himself upright. I helped him to his wabbly pins, fastened the focus on him. His map was plenty messy in the red glow from the fire exit light, but I tabbed him in spite of that.

"Lumpy Valanno!" I said.

He tried to answer me; couldn't. He didn't have enough breath available. Not that he needed to tell me anything about himself. I already knew. During recent months he and his partner in slapstick, Beau Babbitt, had become household words.

ORIGINALLY the team of Babbitt and Valanno had been knockabout comedians in cheap burlesque. Then they had graduated into radio, clicked on the networks with their loony routines. As soon as their Crossley rating skyrocketed high enough, Hollywood had reached out and grabbed them.

First they'd been cast by Superb Pix in a low-budget opus—and the quickie hit the jackpot, coined a fortune. Whereupon Altamount chiseled them away by slipping them a long term starring contract at a staggering stipend. In a sense, it was a raw deal for Superb Pix—but those things happen all the time in the galloping snapshot racket. And now, after cavorting in a couple of lavish Altamount productions, Babbitt and Valanno were on top of the world.

But this didn't explain the assault and bashery just committed on Valanno's pudgy person. As far as I knew, no scandal had ever touched the fat little comic since his advent in Hollywood—no dames, no liquor, no rough stuff. He was just a respectable married guy who'd hit it lucky. Then why the hell had those four masked weasels tried to render him useless?

Remembering something he'd bleated, I thought I might have the answer. I said: "Look, friend. I'm Dan Turner, private snoop. If you need a bodyguard, I'm for hire. Rates reasonable, time and a half for night work, no charge for wasted bullets—if any."

He trembled like a cat coughing lollypops. "No ... oh, my God, it isn't ... I can't have ..."

"Okay, skip it," I shrugged. "At least let me see you home and slap a beefsteak on that shiner."

He sagged against the wall. "I can't go home now. I'm working late on some last-minute retakes for our new picture. I just stepped out in the alley for a breath of fresh air when those men jumped at—" All of a sudden he started to wheeze, deep in his gullet. His mitt clawed at his shirt-front.

I've been around long enough to tab cardiac symptoms when I see them. I plunged at him, propped him up. "Heart?"

He nodded, gasped. His lips were turning blue. "Side pocket—coat—quick!"

I dipped my duke in his duds, came out with a fragile glass ampule. I crushed the tiny thing with my fingers, held it under his battered beezer. He sucked in a deep whiff of the sharp medicinal fumes; a touch of color seeped back into his puss. "Thanks," he whispered hoarsely. "But for God's sake don't tell my wife—she mustn't know the shape I'm in! It would worry her...."

"Sure, sure," I said. "Let's go indoors so you can sit down a while." I steered him to that Altamount fire exit where the red bulb glowed, helped him over the threshold.

Just inside the big sound stage building I gandered a row of dressing rooms. One door had a star on it, with Valanno 's name lettered underneath. I popped the portal open, dumped the beefy bozo on a chair—

Whammo! At first I thought we were having another earthquake. Something soft and fragrant and feminine flurried at me, tripped me to the floor,

*I was too late. The sharp prickle of the knife had sliced through my coat and was resting on my spine.*

landed on top of me. Raking fingernails stabbed at my lamps and a voice throaty with hysteria yeeped: "You dirty gambler's thug—I'll kill you if you've hurt him!"

I SQUIRMED under the chiffon-sheathed stems that straddled me. They were long and tapered and nifty to match the tall slenderness of the wren they belonged to. I said: "What the hell!"

She kept digging for my optics. She was a red-haired wildcat in a dress of clingy rayon that adhered to her delishful contours like sprayed emerald lacquer. Where the skirt had hiked northward, you could pipe creamy skin above the garter line, whiter than any she-male thighs I'd looked at in a month of Mondays. Over me, the surging buoyancy of her mounded breasts made my fingertips itch to go exploring; I couldn't help drawing a thump out of the intimate contact of her body on mine, in spite of her efforts to let the juice out of my eyeballs.

Thump or no thump, I couldn't lie there and let her rake her monogram on my map. I rolled sidewise; bucked like a bronco. She lost her scissors hold; went tumbling across the room. I scrambled to her, nailed her with my poundage. "Hold still, baby!" I panted. "Before I slap the bejaspers out of you!"

"You—you stinking *hood!*"

Over on the other side of the room, Valanno oozed his pudgy form up off the chair. "He's not a hood, Sandra. He's Dan Turner, private detective. He just saved my life, out in the alley." Then he told her what had happened, omitting only the heart-attack part of it. He ended up by saying to me: "Sandra is my wife, Mr. Turner."

I turned her loose and we both scrambled upright. She was a vast, lovely blush from her wavy titian hair to the deep-cut dip of her emerald frock. She pulled a shoulder strap back into place and faltered: "Can y-you ever forgive me? It was such a weird mistake ...!"

"Not so weird," I said. I fished out a gasper, set fire to it. "Especially when you knew in advance that somebody had threatened to lump him up."

She jerked as if I'd jabbed her with a red hot awl. "I—why, I don't understand what you—" The words died on her gorgeous red kisser as the door opened and somebody ankled into the room.

I tabbed this newcomer right away. He was Beau Babbitt, tall, good looking straight-man in the comedy team of Babbitt and Valanno. He said: "Hey, the cameras are waiting ... Migahd, Valanno, what happened to your face?"

"I got in a brawl," the fat guy said. "It won't show if I use enough makeup." He dabbed grease paint on his mauled mush, covered it with powder. "Let's go. Sandra, I'll leave you here with Mr. Turner. I think he deserves an explanation." Then the two comedians hauled bunions.

I grinned at the red-haired chick. "You don't have to explain, baby," I said. "I think I'm hep. To begin with, while your hubby was being manhandled, he kept bleating a promise to pay Shanghai. Then, later, when you hopped me, you called me a gambler's thug. It stacks up to make sense."

"What k-kind of sense, Mr. Turner?"

I said: "The biggest gambling joint in Hollywood right now is Shanghai Mamie's place out on the Sunset Strip. Mamie's got a hardboiled rep where welchers are concerned. She gets her dough or she takes it out of their hides. The way I figure, your ever-loving spouse dropped a cargo of I.O.U.'s to this Shanghai Mamie at one of her games—and then refused to pay off. So she sent a strongarm squad to teach him a lesson."

SANDRA VALANNO drifted closer to me. Her glims looked scared. "Y-yes, Mr. Turner. You've got it right. Only it was a crooked dice game. That's why we didn't want to pay. And then they began sending threats ... and we didn't know what to do. Before we could decide, th-this happened." She made a vague gesture in the general direction of the alley.

Which reminded me of the two rats I'd left out there. I said: "Look. I'll toss that pair of vermin in the gow on an assault rap. That'll show Shanghai Mamie she can't—"

"No! Oh, no, Mr. Turner! You *mustn't!*" One jump put the red-haired mama up against me. She twined her arms around my neck and pasted her gorgeous curves to my brisket. "Please!" Then she fed me a sizzling kiss that blistered me to the insteps.

I gasped like a gaffed flounder. I hadn't expected any such ardent maneuver and it startled the curds out of me. I could feel the yielding surge of soft mounds on my chest; the languorous sway of her ripe hips. It was a hell of a swell sensation—but I didn't savvy the reason for it.

I unfastened myself from her leech-like hold and said: "Wait a minute. What cooks, sweet stuff? How come you don't want Shanghai Mamie's minions in the Bastille?"

"Be-because then the newspapers would know about the gambling debt ... the scandal ..."

I said: "So what?"

"The t-team of Babbitt and Valanno would be washed up in the movies. At least the Valanno part would." She glued herself to me again; bribed me with her glims and kisser and contours. "It—it would be w-worth a lot to m-me if you'd forget the whole thing—pretend it n-never happened!"

That one maverick shoulder strap took another skid off first base; dropped low enough to show

more firm, delicious roundness than was good for my hardened arteries. After all, I'm as human as the next lug—and Sandra Valanno's charms were tempting as hell. I feasted my peepers; couldn't help remembering the thrill I'd got when she had me on the rug a while ago with her legs straddling me....

... "Okay, hon," I said. "You win. I won't call copper. But I think we ought to render some patchwork on those guys out in the alley. I left them in bad shape."

She studied me curiously, her lamps shining. "You'd sooner look after them than stay here with

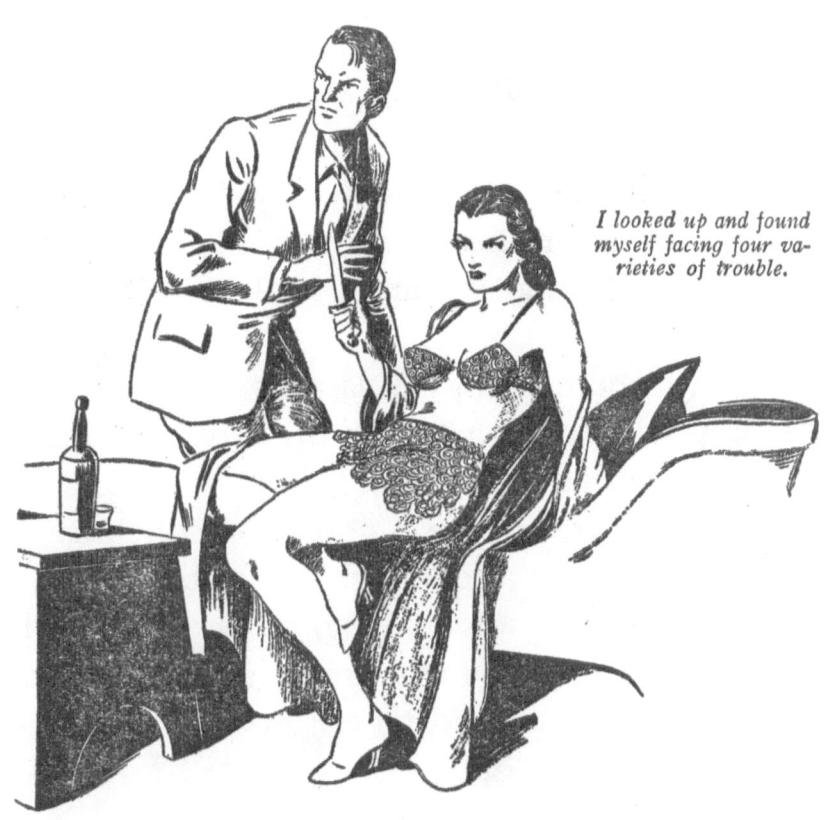

*I looked up and found myself facing four varieties of trouble.*

me? You aren't going to insist on . .?"

I said: "Listen, babe. When a wren loves her hubby as much as you do, so much that you'd be willing to pay off that way to keep him out of the grease—well, nuts! You're the sweetest dish I ever kissed but I've still got a shred of ethics. I'll keep my trap zippered about what happened tonight but I won't take a fee for it. Come on, let's glom a hinge at the alley."

She stood on her tiptoes, gave me a succulent kiss of gratitude. Then the door opened and a voice rumbled: "You filthy son of a witch!"

I WHIRLED; saw Beau Babbitt barging at me with his maulies doubled. "Making love to my partner's wife—!" he rasped.

Sandra blocked him. "You fool! I was j-just thanking him for his promise to keep quiet! He isn't going to tell about Shanghai Mamie, is all. Are you crazy, Beau?"

"Crazy where Lumpy Valanno's concerned, yes. He's my friend. I won't have his wife chiseling on him." His glims scorched her.

I said: "For crysakes, nobody's chiseling. Or would you care for a good stiff swat on the prow?"

When he saw I was leveling, he lost some of his truculence. "Okay. So I was wrong. So I'm sorry." He went to the dresser and picked up his pudgy pal's makeup kit; ankled out.

I looked at the red-haired jenny. "Now that storm's over, how's for a gander at the alley?"

"I'm ready," she said. Her voice didn't even sound ruffled.

We went to the fire exit, opened it, stared outside. The two masked lugs were gone. Either they'd lammed under their own steam or their friends had come back for them. That was jake with me. It took a load off my conscience.

With Sandra hanging onto my arm, I drifted toward the brightly lighted set at the other end of the sound stage building where her porky hubby was working with Beau Babbitt in a retake scene. I wanted to let Valanno know everything was serene; all he had to do was send a check out to Shanghai Mamie's gambling hell and the incident would be washed up. But I never got to tell the little fat guy. He died too soon.

THE SET was dressed to represent an old time wild west barroom somewhere in Arizona on the Fourth of July. According to the scenario, Lumpy Valanno was a low-comedy tenderfoot from the east while Babbitt played the role of a cowboy addicted to practical jokes. Watching from behind the camera lines, I saw Valanno pretending to doze in a rickety chair near the bar with his brogans resting on the rim of a big brass spittoon. The take was under way and the porky guy was giving out with slapsticks snores for the benefit of the sound track.

An assortment of extras and bit players clustered in the background, going through the motions of swilling skee. Beau Babbitt was offstage, waiting for his cue. Presently the director signaled him.

In the shadowy gloom beyond the Kliegs, a prop man handed a small red cylinder to a jane with hair the color of mellow honey. She was the unit's script clerk—and I twitched a little when I tabbed her. Lisbeth Lennord and I had been on many a party in the old days; she was a cute chick and a hell of a good sport. But the last time I'd met her, she'd been a private secretary in the executive department of Superb Pix next door. It seemed funny for her to be clerking for an Altamount unit now. Quite a comedown, in fact. I'd always figured she was in solid as a rock with the big shots at Superb.

But maybe Babbitt and Valanno had brought her over to Altamount with them when they made the jump, I thought. Maybe they'd got acquainted with her, liked her and talked her into throwing in with them. Or it was possible that Superb had fired her and she'd grabbed the first handy berth. Anyhow, here she was on the Babbitt-Valanno set, trig and smart in white linen skirt and a sweater that would have thrown the Hays office censors into a panic. Just looking at the sweater and its alluring contents panicked my own blood pressure.

She accepted the prop man's little red cylinder,

carried it over to Beau Babbitt, gave it to him. He strode onto the set with it; and under the banked lights I saw it was a firecracker. Babbitt went through the pantomime of shushing the extras at the bar. Then he sneaked toward his snoring partner.

I tumbled to the gag. It was a primitive wild west version of the hotfoot. Babbitt slipped the fire-cracker between Valanno's hoof and the cuspidor; wiped a match on his pants and touched fire to the fuse. He backed off to the far end of the stage, jammed his fingers in his ears, screwed his pan into a grimace.

Alongside me, Sandra Valanno whispered: "Watch this. There's a trick spout under that spit-toon. When the firecracker goes off, water will spout up toward Babbitt and those others, drench them. It's a backfire gag, because my husband will go right on snoring—*aeiee-ee-eek!*"

HER scream was a thin thread of sound, almost drowned out by a sharp blast that rattled my ear-drums, jarred my tripes. White-hot flames flashed like a miniature sheet before my glims, flame that erupted from the property firecracker. Only it wasn't a firecracker at all. It must have been loaded with a charge of dynamite.

The explosion was small, vicious, concentrated. I yelled: "What the hell—!" and felt a solid gush of air slamming me off-balance. All around me juicers, cameramen, sound technicians, and assistant directors were scrambling like eggs in an omelette; caterwauling their adenoids out. Dead ahead, the barroom set was a chaotic uproar of overturned props and shouting extras. Lumpy Valanno had been blown off his chair and was flat on his back, not moving. I copped a swivel at his feet and came damned near tossing my cookies. He didn't have any feet. They were mangled, shattered hunks of hamburger.

And now, for a single instant following the blast, there was a silence you could slice like cheese. Everybody was too stunned to say anything. I gulped, got control of my churning elly-bay and went hurtling toward the prone little fat guy; picked up his pudgy left wrist. It was limber in my grasp. I couldn't find a trace of pulse. His kisser was a nasty purple color.

"Get tourniquets!" somebody bleeped. "Bandage his ankles before he bleeds to death! Get a doctor!" Like a wave, people began surging forward.

I straightened up, waved them back. I said: "Tourniquets and doctors won't help. What we need is the homicide squad."

"Homicide—?"

"Yeah. Valanno's deader than fish on Friday. He was bumped."

The defunct guy's red-haired wife—his widow, now—clawed herself through the crush with Beau

Babbitt beside her. "No! No!" she wailed. "I don't believe it!"

Babbitt held her. "Steady, Sandra. He's gone. Somebody tried to cripple him by substituting dynamite for my firecracker—and his bad heart couldn't stand the shock." Then the surviving partner stared at a chunky, ape-shouldered prop man on the fringe of the mob.

I looked too; felt my gullet tightening. That prop man was the one who'd first handled the doctored firecracker before it got to Babbitt—but there was something else about him I thought I recognized.

It was his sniffer. Trickles of claret were leaking out of it; the nostrils looked puffy, inflamed. His peepers seemed somehow familiar, too, as if maybe I'd tabbed them above a handkerchief mask not too long ago. All of a sudden I recalled that brawl in the alley; remembered tapping one masked rodent on the trumpet to give myself a breathing spell while reaching for my roscoe.

NOW I said: "Hey, you!" and pointed a finger at him. "When did you get that smack on the smeller?"

He touched it, looked at his palm, saw the wet redness. He stiffened. "Why—why, I g-guess the concussion did it when that thing exploded. My nose bleeds easily—"

I lunged at him. "Like hell. You were one of the four dastards that put the boots to Valanno in the alley a while back!"

He edged off. "What—?"

"Yeah!" I snarled. "You're one of Shanghai Mamie's triggers, bi-gahd! The one that piped my badge and lammed!" I flicked out my handcuffs, stabbed them at his mitts.

He ducked, swerved, came up with a rung of the chair that Valanno had been sitting on when the blast went off. It was hard and heavy. He balanced it like a baseball bat, swung it, wrapped it around my noggin.

Neon lights pinwheeled through my think-tank. I felt myself falling; couldn't keep the floor from drifting up at me, slugging me on the puss. I took a trip to dreamland.

I WOKE up with the raw taste of rye in my mouth. I hate rye. It's too damned peppery on your tonsils. "Scotch is my tipple," I gargled. Then I pried my fuzzy lamps open, stared up into the beefy lineaments of my friend Dave Donaldson, homicide lieutenant.

Dave's headquarters minions were all over the stage like a herd of termites. Evidently I'd remained under ether for quite a while after their advent, because Lumpy Valanno's remnants had already been carted off to the morgue and most of the extras and bit players dismissed. Now Donaldson pulled his flash away from my kisser and said: "I'll hand it to you, Sherlock. You must have a cast iron skull."

I sat up, touched the sore place. There was a knot on my dome the size of an alarm clock. Over its dull throbbing I could hear a series of feminine whimpers, sobbing, muffled. That was Sandra Valanno on the other side of the stage, mournful as a red-haired Niobe, refusing to be comforted by Beau Babbitt's awkward efforts. She didn't even seem to realize he was trying.

Looking at his strained expression, I could guess how he was feeling. It must have been tough for him to know it was his match that had touched off the jazzed-up firecracker. I couldn't quite decide which one to be sorrier for: the jane because she had lost her hubby or Babbitt because he'd been the instrument of his partner's demise. I wound up by just feeling sorry for myself because my noggin hurt so bad.

I wabbled to my pins, fastened the foggy focus on Donaldson. "Did you nab the guy that maced me?"

"No. The dragnet's out for him, though. I got his name; Pete Hinshaw. They tell me you accused him of being a torpedo for Shanghai Mamie so I sent a squad out to her joint."

That scalded me. Anybody with an ounce of grey matter should know Shanghai Mamie's gambling dive was the last place on earth the ape-shouldered prop man would use for a hideout. It was too damned obvious. If he got any shelter from Mamie, it would be in a much safer place. Her private apartment, for instance. That was in the Gayboy Arms on Wilshire and not many people knew about it.

I was one of the few—and I kept the information to myself. I had a personal score to settle with this Hinshaw louse. I owed him a lump on the crock like the one he'd dealt me; and I was in the right mood to deliver it. Later the cops could have him, but not until I got in my licks first.

So I told Dave Donaldson I felt terrible and wished to drag ankles. He tipped me the nod and I took a powder to my rambling wreck. But instead of heading for home I aimed my radiator toward Wilshire Boulevard and the Gayboy Arms.

It was a short haul. I parked, barged into the lobby, grabbed an automatic elevator and thumbed the pent-house button. Presently I was mauling my knuckles on the door of Shanghai Mamie's lavish private layout.

A YEAR had gone down the hatch since my last visit there, but Mamie still had the same cute little slant-eyed maid—a nifty Asiatic dish with white satin pajamas on her curves and drowsiness in her almond glims. "Why, Mr. Turner!" she said.

"Where's Mamie?"

"I—I'm not sure she—"

"Look," I said. I put my hands on the front of her

pajama coat; pushed against softness. "You get Mamie for me or I'll pinch you full of abscesses."

Before she could say anything to that, a voice spoke up from inside. It was a husky voice, like the purr of a tabby-cat. "Let him in, Lotus. Hello, gumshoe. Slumming?"

I drifted over the threshold, sank my tootsies heel deep in plush carpet. The maid lammed and I was all alone with Shanghai Mamie—which is the same as saying I was alone in a cage full of tigers. I broke open a fresh deck of pills, got one going.

"Hiya, Toots," I said through the smoke.

Mamie wasn't what you might have expected of a White Russian jane from the Orient. That description usually makes you picture a stately, regal-looking mama with a hardboiled puss and a shiv in her garter. But Mamie was just the opposite. She was tiny, like a fragile doll. Her hair was drawn back in a sleek midnight bun at the nape of her gorgeous neck; she didn't wear a speck of makeup on her Madonna map. A quilted Chinese robe draped her from throat to ankles, completely hiding her dainty curves. And yet, in spite of that, you knew the curves were there. You sensed them—along with the aura of danger that cloaked her like an invisible warning. She was dynamite.

She smiled at me—and I got goose pimples on my spine as big as jellybeans. Mamie was deadpan except when something annoyed her. That was the only time she ever smiled. She was smiling now. I had a sudden attack of jabber-wockies.

She said: "It's been a long time, Hawkshaw. Have a drink?" She glided to a cellarette, produced a fifth of Vat 69. She had a damned good memory. She knew my preference.

"Thanks, no," I told her. "I'm here on business. I want Pete Hinshaw."

"Hinshaw. Do I know him?"

I said: "Yeah. He's a prop man for Altamount. He's also one of your bully boys. Let's not horse, hon. You're hep to the score. This is murder you're fooling around with now."

She stretched out on a deep-cushioned divan and the quilted robe slid open just enough to show a hint of ivory gams, a peep at perfect little flesh-treasures nestling in a gossamer bandeau. "I don't know what you're talking about," she purred. "Come here. Sit by me. Tell me you're sorry you've neglected me so long."

I perched my heft on the divan's edge; got set to wrap my dukes around her lovely gullet if she tried anything funny. "You aren't kidding me, sweet stuff."

"Stop talking riddles. Be nice to me. Or have you forgotten how?"

"I never forget. I'm just not in the mood, is all. Hinshaw bent a chair rung around my conk a while ago. It drained me."

*"Hold still, baby," I panted, "before I slap you silly."*

"Poor Dan." She touched my noggin. Then her arms tangled me and she draw me downward, pulled my mush toward hers. Her kisser was parted, red, moist. The quilted robe gave up the struggle and fluttered all the way open.

I gasped: "Jeest—*hey, damn you to hell!*" But I was too late. She had me. I was locked tight in a jiujitsu hold; felt the sharp prickle of a knife-point cutting through the back of my coat to rest against my spine. That was going to cost me a tailor's bill to get the hole sewed up.

Mamie's glims mocked me. She raised her furry voice. "Pete. Come here. Bring your boys."

FOOTFALLS sounded behind me. Somebody yanked me off the divan, slammed me against the wall. I blinked and found myself facing four varieties of trouble.

Pete Hinshaw, the ape-shouldered prop man, was one. So I'd been right in thinking I'd find him here. It was small satisfaction, though. The three guys flanking him were the ones from the alley back of Altamount Studios; the rats who'd pasted hell out of Lumpy Valanno. I tabbed two of them from the condition of their pans, the marks of my own dukes. Now, evidently, it was going to be their turn.

Hinshaw rubbed his inflamed smeller. "Hello, snoop."

"Hello, killer."

He scowled. "Don't call me that, wise guy. You did it once on the sound stage. You know what it bought you."

Shanghai Mamie glided forward. "You're an awful dope, Dan. First you butted into something that was none of your business—a little matter of teaching Valanno he shouldn't welch on his bets. And then later, when he happened to get chilled, you tried to pin it on an innocent man."

"So Hinshaw's innocent," I said. "Who told you?"

"He did. I believe him, Apparently you disagree. That's too bad, Dan. It's going to cost you a lot of trouble." She turned to Hinshaw and his buddies. "All right, boys. Let him have it. Keep remembering all he's done to you—and don't pull your punches." Her dark peepers were glowing and she raised her hands to her tiny breasts; pressed them flat as if to quiet the pulsations that made them surge against the brassiere.

I said: "You brazen little sadist!" and made a lunge at her. She side-stepped; and then a fist bounced off my whiskers, damned near caved in my bowsprit. That made another debt I owed to Pete Hinshaw.

But this was no time to think about paying it. I knew I was in for a larruping if I stayed on my feet. So I walled back my optics, let my gams sag. I hit the rug. I didn't move.

I heard Mamie saying:. "You idiot. I wanted him mussed up, not cold-corked. No use kicking him. He wouldn't feel it. Get out."

"Out—?" That was Hinshaw sounding startled.

"Yes, out. For all we know, the cops may be following this bright boy. You mustn't be found here, any of you."

Hinshaw said: "So what if they do find us? I keep telling you I don't know anything about that dynamite firecracker. If there was a switch in my props, it happened while my back was turned. . . Cripes! Wait a minute! I just thought of something!"

*I clipped her on the button and a dribble of froth, like steam, came out of her mouth.*

"You haven't got what it takes to think," Shanghai Mamie's voice sounded vicious with disappointment. My quick fold-up had frustrated her out of a cargo of thrills. "What is it you think you're thinking?"

"That honey-haired wren," Hinshaw said. "That script clerk. The one with the sweater full of oomph. Lisbeth Lennord, her name is."

"Well?"

"She could have switched that firecracker. I gave it to her first, then she passed it to Babbitt. Maybe she handed him a different one."

"Why?"

"Well, look. She used to be in thick with the biggies over at Superb. You know, where Babbitt and

Valanno were before Altamount chiseled them away."

"And—?"

"Suppose those guys over at Superb were sore at losing their comedy gold mine. Suppose they planted this Lennord bim with Altamount for a revenge stunt? Like maybe crippling Valanno—so the team would be busted up. Only they didn't know the fat slob had a bum ticker, any more than we knew it when we belted him around."

"I think you're nuts," Mamie said. I wanted to shout agreement but I didn't dare. If I let them know I was conscious, they'd kick the bejoseph out of me. All the same, I knew this Pete Hinshaw was just trying to rig a fall guy so he'd be out from under the murder rap himself. Only when he picked Lisbeth Lennord he was watering the wrong stump. I knew her too damned well to consider her as a suspect.

Hinshaw growled: "Okay, so I'm nuts. But suppose I drop in to see this Lennord jessie? Suppose I happen to find some left-over dynamite in her stash?"

"By planting it there?" Shanghai Mamie said.

"Hell. Maybe I wouldn't have to. Maybe I could twist a confession outa her."

MAMIE'S voice perked up. "That would be nice. You could bring her here so I'd be able to watch. I think I'd like that." Her tone droped to a purr again. "But first there's another job."

"Yeah? What?"

"Go see Beau Babbitt and Mrs. Valanno. Tell them we want our money."

"But it was Valanno that owed us—"

"He is dead. They are alive. As far as I'm concerned, they're responsible for the debt. If necessary, we'll use ... persuasion."

"Listen, Mamie. You know I'm red hot right now on account of Valanno getting chilled. I can't—"

"On your way. All of you. Get that money. Then see about this Lennord girl. Handle her properly and you won't be red hot with the cops. Move, now!"

I heard them pad-padding across the rug's deep piling; then a door opened, closed again. I took a chance, opened my windows, gave forth with a hollow groan. I also bit a chunk out of the inside of my cheek so a worm of crimson would streak down over my chin. Shanghai Mamie was goofy over gore.

She came to me; dropped to her knees. I could smell the perfume of her hair, the warmth of her body. She was breathing fast. "Dan, honey ..."

I said: "Aw, *nuts!*" made a loose fist and clipped her on the button. A dribble of froth came out of her mouth, like steam. She relaxed.

I jumped up, shivered and got the hell out of there.

MY HEAP can wind up eighty in an emergency. I

souped it to ninety, going out Wilshire. Pete Hinshaw and his three henchmen had a ten-minute start on me already. If they got to Sandra Valanno and did anything dirty to her, I promised myself I'd take them apart inch by inch, strew them all over the precinct. I liked that red-haired wren; liked the memory of the pash-bribe she'd tried to give me in her hubby's dressing room to save him from scandal. Now that Valanno was deceased, she needed somebody to look after her. And I was the guy for the job.

There was another cutie involved: Lisbeth Lennord, the honey-haired script clerk with the sweater full of lure. I liked her, too. But she was second on Hinshaw's list of calls to be made tonight. She could wait. After all, I'm not twins.

The Valanno tepee was a fairly modest Spanish-modern layout just this side of Beverly. I made it without turning up any motorcycle bulls, which was a miracle at the speed I was going. Every time I rounded a corner my tires sang soprano.

Pretty soon I tossed out my anchors, skidded to a shuddering stop. I slapped my brogans up a flight of terraced steps, gained the tiled front patio, leaned on the bell push.

Lights came on in the entrance hall. The door opened. Lumpy Valanno's widow stared at me. "Mr. Turner—!"

I said: "Thank God you're okay, kiddo."

Then I spotted Beau Babbitt standing behind the curvesome red-haired cupcake.

He scowled at me. "What made you think she might not be okay?" he wanted to know.

"Because a detachment of Shanghai Mamie's thugs are on their way here with malice afore-thought," I said. "Mamie wants her dough. The geetus Valanno should have paid her."

Babbitt rubbed his cheek. It was fiery red; you could see the clear outlines of fingerprints against his shave. "Shanghai Mamie's men have already. been here. They're gone."

I said: "What?"

"Y-yes, Mr. Turner," Sandra said dully. "They m-made threats. So we p-promised to send them the money."

"I promised," Babbitt corrected her gently. "I have enough annuities laid aside to take care of us the rest of our lives, even though I never make an-other picture." He started to slide an arm around the red-haired babe's slender waist, then seemed to re-consider it. I guess he just remembered her hubby was fresh dead.

I peered at the fingermarks on his puss. "You get slugged a little, friend?"

"One of them hit me in the face, yes."

I said: "They play rough," and turned to Sandra; smiled into her tense expression. "Where's a phone? I've got to call the gendarmes."

She pointed. I picked the handset out of its cradle, dialed headquarters. I asked for homicide, got Dave Donaldson. I said: "Turner talking. Listen fast. I was right about that prop man being on Shanghai Mamie's payroll."

"Pete Hinshaw, you mean?"

"Yeah, Hinshaw. He and three sluggers are on their way right now to pull a snatch. A jenny named Lisbeth Lennord is their meat. She—"

"I know her. Script clerk on that Babbitt-Valanno unit. I interviewed her on the set, turned her loose."

I said: "For the love of What'sHis-Name, will you quit interrupting me? Here's the lowdown. Lisbeth Lennord used to work for Superb Pix. Superb is the studio that lost Babbitt and Valanno to Altomount. Lisbeth is one of the people who handled that doctored firecracker tonight. So now this Pete Hinshaw is going to put the snatch on her, try to bop a confession out of her—make her admit Superb bribed her to plant the explosive."

"So that's it!" Dave roared. "I never thought of that angle! You think Hinshaw's right, Philo?"

I said: "How the hell should I know? The point is, you can round up the whole damned works if you move fast. Otherwise the Lennord gal is liable to get her profile bashed. Know where she lives? Good. Meet me there—and get the lead out of your frame." I rang off, made for Sandra Valanno's front door.

Beau Babbitt blocked me. He looked grimmer

than a carload of caskets. "I couldn't help hearing what you said, Turner. And I'm going with you. If that Lennord witch killed my partner, I'm going to be on deck when she's nailed to the cross."

"Me too," Sandra said quietly.

I told them that was okay with me. We bounced out to my bucket, piled in. I kicked my cylinders to life, stoked them up past the safety zone. We went away from there in a shower of dust.

LISBETH LENNORD lived alone in a self-effacing bungalow near Yucca and Argyle. I blistered the asphalt, cut a screeching hole in the night. By the time we got to our destination my jalopy was bleeding steam from every pore.

When I parked I noticed another heap already at the curb, a black sedan that somehow reminded me of an undertaker 's hearse although it didn't actually look like one except in my imagination. I guess it was my knowledge of the honey-haired script clerk's jeopardy that gave me the impression. Anyhow I knew Pete Hinshaw and his pals were on the job, and got to the Lennord frill's stash ahead of me. It wasn't just a hunch, either. I could hear a faint she-male yeep from inside. It spelled trouble.

I slung myself to the pavement, raced for the porch. Beau Babbitt was on my heels but I said: "Get back. Take care of Sandra. There may be shooting— and these lads don't carry cap pistols." Then I hit

Lisbeth Lennord's front portal with my hurtling beef.

It splintered inward. I yanked out my heater, thumbed off the safety catch. Then I went blamming into the living room. I rasped: "Lay off before I start spraying poison out of this Flit gun."

THE tableau in front of me was something to remember. Hinshaw, the ape-shouldered property man, had the Lennord quail up against a wall. He was backed by his three burly bullies—not that he needed them for what he was doing to the chick with the ripe honey hair. Hinshaw was the kind that could cop the duke over a woman any day in the week.

He had ripped Lisbeth's sweater open from neck to Nebraska, likewise snagging her brassiere in the process. Now that fragile embellishment hung in peek-a-boo tatters over skin that was like peaches and cream. There were bruises marring her snowy shoulders; her glims were deep azure pools of fear. Her unpent coiffure streamed like a golden waterfall around her white throat and down on her throbbing charms—and the vision of velvety epidermis peeping through a mist of yellow tresses thrilled me to the shoestrings.

But the bruises made me see eleven shades of red. I tapped a tattoo on Hinshaw's spine with my lift mitt, kept his three chums covered with the rod in my right. "Turn, bud," I said.

He let go of the wren, spun to face me. I corked him square on the sore nostrils with a left hook. Twin streams of gravy made a mess of his necktie. "Damn you to hell—!" he whined.

I said: "That's just interest on the debt I owe you, cousin. The worst is yet to come."

"You can't—"

I popped him again, just to show him how wrong he was. When his pals stirred I waved my gat at them. "Freeze, all of you. Unless you hanker to have yourselves air conditioned."

Hinshaw's cheeks twitched. "Listen. snooper. Let's talk this over."

"Talk won't help," I said. I flicked a glance at Lisbeth Lennord. "Go sit down, babe. Tell me how far these illegitimates went with you before I arrived."

She sank into a chair, tried to pull the sweater shut over her delishful breasts where they swelled ripely out of the torn place. "They j-just hit me, is all. And Hinshaw ripped m-my clothes. . . ."

"Nothing else?"

She blushed. "N-no. Except he—he accused me of switching that property firecracker for one with a charge of high explosive in it."

"Guilty or innocent, hon?"

"Innocent, of course! I wouldn't—"

FROM behind me a flat voice said: "*Somebody did it.*

*Somebody* gave Beau Babbitt the one that killed my husband." That was Sandra Valanno coming into the room. She had Babbitt with her. I suppose they'd got tired of waiting out in my coupe.

Pete Hinshaw copped a hinge at the hatred that glittered in the red-haired widow's peepers. "It wasn't me, lady!" he whined. "Honest to God it wasn't. Yeah, I admit me and the boys gave your old man a pasting. But that was something else. We didn't have a damned thing to do with that fire-cracker switch."

"You say," Beau Babbitt growled.

"I say. And I'm leveling. Why the hell do you think we came here to see this Lennord bim?"

"To frame her," I lifted a lip.

"Ix-nay, shamus. To make her yodel the truth. *She* handled the firecracker after I did. *She* gave it to Babbitt. Why, the filthy little slut's guilty as hell!"

I whopped him across the mouth. "Watch your language, punk. And if you've got any accusations to make, wait until the bulls get here. Make it official."

"Here—the bulls? God!" he cringed.

Beau Babbitt rasped: "Look, Turner. We're wasting a lot of time. Why don't you search the house, see if you find anything that might incriminate Miss Lennord?"

"You make the frisk." I said. "I'm busy keeping these guys covered."

Babbitt began like an amateur. Lisbeth Lennord

crouched dully in a chair; watched him with apathetic lamps. Presently she choked: "Wh-what do you expect to find?"

He picked up her pocketbook from a corner table, got it open, looked inside. Then his map contorted. He breathed: "By heaven, this is what I expected to find!" And he held up a small crimson cylinder. A firecracker.

For a split second everybody got so quiet you could hear a change in the climate. Then hell boiled over. Pete Hinshaw bellowed: "That's it! That's the original prop! Now I see what happened! I gave it to this Lennord broad and she switched it, put it in her purse, handed Babbitt a phoney charged with dynamite! Come on, boys—let's blow!"

And he splashed himself at the door with his three pals trailing him like tails to a comet.

I'd been so interested in the firecracker that the move almost caught me with my rompers at half mast. But not quite. I've got quick reflexes. I barreled across the room, body-blocked the prop man, fetched him a jolt on the haircut with the muzzle end of my cannon. That bashed him into his buddies and they all went down like a tangle of pretzels. One of them managed to pull his roscovitch. He aimed it at me.

From the doorway, Dave Donaldson's voice rumbled like thunder with sandpaper on it. "Target practice. Just what I've been needing." A service .38

yammered: "Ka-*chow!*" and the guy on the floor dropped his heater, fixed the stupid focus on his shattered wrist. Then Dave and a handful of homicide heroes lumbered into the room.

I said: "Thanks, girls. You're just in time."

DONALDSON beetled his brows. "In time for what?"

"The blowoff," I said. "This cleans up the Valanno kill."

Pete Hinshaw pushed himself off the rug. "You can't pin that on me! I'm just a prop man—"

"But you carry Shanghai Mamie 's sideline," I told him. "Criminal assaults wrapped up to take home."

"That's not murder! I—"

I said: "Skip it." Then I looked at Lisbeth Lennord. "About that firecracker in your bag, hon."

"Dan ... my God, please ... you don't really believe I did that, surely... ? She trembled toward me, forgot to hold that torn sweater together. Her creamy, mounded breasts heaved up and down with her gasped breathing. Her puss was as pale as milk from an anemic cow.

I had a hell of an impulse to grab her, maul her quiet—but I don't always obey my impulses. I said: "Back off and pipe down, sis. I'll do the talking now."

Dave Donaldson grumbled: "Then do it. Before I blow my topper."

"Okay," I said. "Lumpy Valanno's croaking was premeditated—by somebody who knew he had a faulty pump. Understand, the doctored firecracker wasn't loaded heavily enough to blow Valanno dead. That would have endangered everybody else on the set. But it carried just enough of a charge to shock the little fat guy's ticker out of action."

Donaldson gave me the fishy glimpse. "Come on, Sherlock. Pull your rabbit out of the hat."

I gave myself a gasper, set it afire. I said: "A short while ago I went over to the Altamount lot." This was a lie, but I had a damned good reason for it. "I had them run me a rush projection of the scene where Valanno was cooled. Just as I expected, the camera caught somebody in the act of turning away from the blast, ducking before it went off."

Sandra Valanno grabbed my arm. Her pinkies sank into me so hard I could hear my marrow squishing. She said: "But that—that would mean—"

"Yeah. This party knew what force to expect out of the explosion. And it was the same guy who planted the real firecracker in Lisbeth Lennord's purse just now—the original firecracker which he'd had in his pocket ever since he switched it for the doctored duplicate, back on the set. We'll prove that scientifically by microscope examination of the dust from his pocket. His will be the only duds to show gunpowder dust—hey, Dave! There he goes! *Nab Beau Babbitt!*"

THE tall and handsome straight man in the late lamented comedy team of Babbitt and Valanno was already on his way to the nearest window. When I yelped, he wheeled. He had a gun in his mitt. He cut loose with it.

*Her hair felt soft, silky, smelled nice.*

I cut loose with mine first; splintered his right kneecap. His chattering rod hosed slugs all over the room as he went down in a cursing heap.

Donaldson lunged at him, kicked the gun away. "That'll cost you, brother."

"You—damn you—you'll never prove—"

I said: "Maybe I couldn't have proved anything. But I ran a hell of a good bluff—and you gave yourself away. *Dead* away, if you consider the gas chamber where you'll wind up," I added.

"You can't send me to the gas chamber for trying to shoot my way ... out of a ... lousy... frameup...!

"Not if your bullets had gone wild. But glom a gander. You just croaked two of Shanghai Mamie's hoods—including her pet crippler, Pete Hinshaw."

"God ... oh, my God...."

I said: "Your scheme to brown Lumpy Valanno was plenty nifty. You figured nobody would suspect you of bumping your partner. In fact, people would be sorry for you because you'd been slipped a dynamite cracker causing his decease. That was nice thinking. But I began to get hep when I remembered a few things."

"Such ... as ...?

"Your jealousy when you caught Valanno's wife dishing me a little kiss. That didn't register with me at first; but it jostled my think-tank later. When I called at Sandra's wikiup a while ago, you had red fingermarks on your mush. You said Shanghai Mamie's boys had bopped you. I know you were lying. Shanghai Mamie's hired hands never slap. They punch—with their fists."

"W-well...?"

"You had been slapped, hard. Nobody was with you except Sandra herself. So I doped it out that you must have made a pass at her and got a stinger across the map."

The red-haired widow said: "You—you're right, Mr. Turner. He *did* try to m-make love to me!"

"So there was the motive," I concluded. I blew smoke in Babbitt's twisted kisser. "You were in love with your partner's wife. You wanted her so damned badly you were willing to cool him, put him out of the way for keeps. You admitted as much when you said you had enough annuity geetus stashed away to take care of Sandra and yourself even if you never made another pic. That proved you were hoping to marry her when things died down.

"So I set a little trap for you. I let you overhear my phone conversation with Lieutenant Donaldson concerning the possibility of Lisbeth Lennord's guilt. I knew you'd insist on coming here to her joint with me. I figured you'd try to plant the firecracker on her. And now your cook is goosed."

He stared past me; glued his glassy gaze on the voluptuous red-haired Valanno widow. "I did it ... for you ... I was crazy over you ... I had to...."

Sandra Valanno cleared her throat. She dredged

up a chunk of phlegm. She spat it in his face.

Then she turned around and walked out.

AFTER the prisoners and cops and corpses were gone, I found myself alone with Lisbeth Lennord. She said: "Dan ... oh-h-h, Dan, how can I ever thank you enough? How can I p-pay you?"

I ran my fingers through her mellow-honey colored hair. It felt soft, silky; smelled nice. "I've got special fees for script clerks, kiddo," I said.

# TO THE READER

**TO THE** reading lover, an interesting, entertaining book is a bargain at any price—their problem being one of finding the right book to suit their personal taste—the kind of story that offers the most reading enjoyment.

Variety is essential to reading pleasure. And the publishers of **FICTION HOUSE PRESS BOOKS** make every effort to provide the widest possible selection for the discriminating reader.

Under the **FICTION HOUSE** imprint appear westerns, romantic novels, thrilling mystery and detective stories, haunting tales of the supernatural, adventure and science fiction—entertaining escape from the everyday world.

You will always find your greatest reading satisfaction under the distinctive imprint of **FICTION HOUSE PRESS** books.

Find the **Fiction House Press Library** online at:

## www.FictionHousePress.com

www.ingramcontent.com/pod-product-compliance
Lightning Source LLC
Chambersburg PA
CBHW060345030726
47497CB00003B/598